Miracle

a novella

K. L. McKee

Cameo Mountain Press
Palisade, CO 81526

First Edition

Scripture quotations are from THE HOLY BIBLE,
THOMPSON CHAIN-REFERENCE® NEW
INTERNATIONAL VERSION®, NIV® Copyright © 1982, by
THE B. B. KIRKBRIDE BIBLE COMPANY, INC. and THE
ZONDERVAN CORPORATION. Used by permission. All
rights reserved worldwide.

Love Will Keep Us Together—words and music by Neil Sedaka
and Howard Greenfield
The Best Gift—words and music by Lan O'Kun

Dedication

To my husband, Steve, who unfailingly believed in me. He endured countless lonely nights as I secluded myself in my office and painstakingly put ideas into tangible words. He is my miracle.

Acknowledgements

My deepest appreciation to Jane Healy, Pamela Larson, Lucinda Stein, Brenda Evers, Pattie Hill, Joyce Anderson, and Donna Bettencourt who've encouraged me, critiqued my writing, and challenged me to be a better writer. And to Father John Farley for his insights.

A special acknowledgement to Virginia LaCrone, teacher and friend, who is now with our Lord in heaven. Her spiritual guidance and lessons in grammar will never be forgotten.

MIRACLE

a novella

"Towards the North shall appear,

Not far from Cancer, a blazing star,

Suza, Sienna, Boetia, Eretrion,

There shall die at Rome a great man, the

night being past. "

Nostradamus

Century 6, Quatrain 6

"Your sons and daughters will prophesy, your old

men will dream dreams, your young men will see

visions . . . . I will show wonders in the heavens . . ."

Joel 2:28, 30a

~1~

January 6, 2014

Los Angeles, California

Gabe paced before the bank of television sets in Sears awaiting the evening news. At the end of the aisle he turned, narrowly missed an errant three-year-old, and stepped aside for the child's frazzled mother. The man he expected, a priest, appeared and turned toward a big screen model.

Gabe smoothed a hand over his thinning gray hair and focused his attention as the news began. He endured the anchorwoman's report of another drive-by shooting in Los Angeles and other local news stories. His impatience grew as the pretty brunette related news from around the world—the killing of 30 people by Islamic gunmen in Nigeria, a terrorist bombing in Israel, and the latest death toll in Syria.

"Come on, get on with it before he leaves," Gabe mumbled as the weatherman reported on the winter storms ravaging New England and Eastern Canada. He positioned himself to subtly block the priest working his way to the exit.

"Excuse me," the priest said.

"Not at all," Gabe replied and moved aside.

"And finally," the anchorwoman intoned, "the Los Angeles Archdiocese announced today the death of Father Lucas Ramirez."

The priest stopped and turned toward the television.

The camera moved in for a closer shot of the anchorwoman's somber face. "Father Ramirez," she continued, "was renowned for what some religious leaders called his scholarly and thought-provoking interpretations of the books of the Bible, particularly the New Testament. A popular author and lecturer, he was perhaps best known for his controversial book *The Second Millennium and the Church.*

"In his book, Father Ramirez predicted only two popes would follow Pope John Paul II, and that in the first quarter of the second millennium, and I quote, 'a child will be born to a man of God and a barren woman. The child will become a great leader, bringing justice, peace, and a new era of hope to the world.' In a recent interview, Father Ramirez stated he would not live to see the birth of the child. A spokesman for the Los Angeles Archdiocese refused further comment concerning Father Ramirez or his prophecy, stating Father Ramirez died quietly in his sleep. Father Ramirez was eighty-three."

"Now it begins," Gabe whispered. He glanced up at the tall priest struggling to regain his composure. Gabe dipped his head in a knowing nod, turned and walked away.

Father Joseph Connor tuned out the remaining newscast and wiped the moisture from his eyes with his fingertips. He had stopped at Sears to pick up a new hammer. On his way out, the news beckoned to him and he stopped to listen. The news of Father Ramirez' death blindsided him.

He'd met Father Ramirez a few months earlier at a lecture. The meeting unsettled Father Joe. He still hadn't sorted out his feelings over comments the respected priest had made to him. More disturbing, Father Joe realized, was that Father Ramirez had appeared vibrant and healthy. Father Joe couldn't believe the man whose writings he respected and studied was dead.

Surely Father Ramirez hadn't outlived his usefulness to God. Or did his sudden death indicate his prophecy would come true? He had been right about other events he'd predicted.

Father Joe said a brief prayer for Father Ramirez' soul. His cell phone interrupted his thoughts. After a brief comment to the caller, he set aside his grief. He was needed elsewhere.

~2~

March 2014

Grand Junction, Colorado

Without a sound, Father Joe set his suitcase inside the hospital room door. The bed near the door was empty, its white sheets and thin beige blanket smoothed tight and tucked into the sides, awaiting its next occupant. He took a deep breath and rubbed his sleep-deprived eyes. Unstable weather had jostled the plane the entire flight from Los Angeles.

Beth Stevens sat next to the far bed, her back to the door. Her hands held another's, the woman barely recognizable with tubes and monitors attached, blinking and beeping their endless rhythm. Beth's forehead rested on both their hands. From the doorway, Joe studied Beth for a moment, the dim light highlighting the strands of her short auburn hair. The last time he had seen her, he had come home to help bury her parents. Now death had brought them together again. He closed his eyes and fought back tears.

She took a deep breath and lifted her head, turning slowly. She smiled when she saw him. "Joe," she said, barely above a whisper. Beth rose to meet him.

His heart turned over. Eight years was a long time not to see an old and precious friend. His choice.

Time left her looking younger and more beautiful
than he remembered. He could see tears in her eyes as
she reached up to hug him. Wrapping his arms around
her, he buried his face against her hair and held her.
Her tears felt warm against his neck. After a few
moments, she gently pushed away and stepped back.

"She's been awake off and on, waiting for you
to come," Beth said. "I don't think she's in much pain.
The doctor has seen to it that she's comfortable." Beth
stepped aside. "Would you like to sit with her? I
never know how long she'll sleep, but I try to make
sure she's not alone when she wakes up."

"Thank you," he murmured.

Joe sat down and reached for his mother's
hand. She's so frail and helpless, he thought. Not at
all like the robust woman who had shaped his life,
encouraged him, reprimanded him, and loved him.
How many times had he sat with the dying, offering

words of comfort and hope? Yet when he needed the words for his mother, he could not find them.

What would he say to her when she awoke and looked into his eyes? She'd had such high expectations for her son, convinced he was destined to achieve greatness by serving God in a special way. He had not only let her down, he had accomplished nothing great.

He prayed, asking God to relieve her suffering and care for her soul. Tears slid down Joe's cheeks as he gave in to grief. He had followed his destiny and worked tirelessly at his calling, but lately, he felt the demands on him were more than he could handle. For every child he saved, five others slipped from his grasp.

Her eyelids fluttered, and she stirred. Joe squeezed her hand and smoothed her bangs away from her forehead.

"Mom, I'm here."

Those were the only words he could manage. He thought he saw her smile, but it might have been his imagination. The soft touch on his shoulder drew his eyes from his mother to look at Beth.

"I'm going down to the cafeteria to get something to eat," she said. "If you need me, the nurses will find me."

He nodded and smiled.

"May I bring you anything?"

"No. I'm fine." He squeezed the hand still resting on his shoulder. "Thank you, again, for being here for her. It means so much to me."

"Think nothing of it, Joe. I love her, too."

~3~

*I*n the hospital cafeteria, Beth lingered over her half-eaten bowl of soup. She had little appetite, but she wanted to give Joe time alone with his mother. She couldn't believe Helen was dying. Barely six weeks ago, Helen sat under the mural at the library enthralling children and their parents with her lively storytelling at family story hour. Beth rested her forehead on her hands and closed her eyes, hoping to shut out the pain in her heart and the look in Joe's eyes when he entered his mother's hospital room.

Helen Connor had been Beth's neighbor and friend since before she could remember. Beth never knew Helen's husband, a policeman who had been killed trying to stop an enraged husband from beating his wife. Helen was pregnant with Joe at the time. She never remarried.

As a child, Beth stayed with Helen and Joe when her parents needed a babysitter. Joe was five years older than Beth, and like any five-year-old, he could not always be bothered with entertaining a baby. Joe would sometimes play with Beth when she was older, but more often than not, he ignored her.

Beth lifted her head and smiled. Joe had been so indifferent to her when she was little, but she looked up to him like she would a brother. Since she had no siblings, he was a perfect substitute. She stopped seeing him as a big brother when she started first grade, the year he became her knight in shining armor.

Beth's house was five blocks from the elementary school. The beginning week of first grade, her mother walked her to school. The second week, Beth's parents trusted her to walk to school by herself. She was three blocks from home her first day on her own when Billy Adams started teasing her. She tried to ignore the obnoxious fourth-grader, but he refused to stop pestering her. Every time she tried to hit him, hoping to chase him off, he ducked, and she punched air. Frustration surfaced in tears.

"Crybaby," Billy chanted. "Crybaby, crybaby, crybaby."

"Stop it!" Beth screamed.

Billy grinned. "Here, crybaby," he sneered as he knocked her lunch pail from her hands. "Now you've got something to cry about."

"Pick it up," came Joe's firm command. He had appeared from nowhere and taken up her cause.

Billy's laughter died in his throat at the look in Joe's eyes. Billy picked up the lunch pail and handed it to Beth.

"Now apologize and promise you won't ever do it again," Joe ordered Billy.

"I-I'm sorry and I won't do it again," Billy stammered.

"Now get out of here." Joe turned to Beth. "Did he hurt you?"

"N-no." Beth stared, unable to believe Joe had come to her rescue.

"Okay. Then dry your eyes. Nobody likes a kid who can't suck it up and be tough. Come on, I'll walk you the rest of the way."

Beth did as she was told, and every morning following the incident, Joe waited at his gate to walk her to school. By the time he was old enough to drive, Joe gave Beth a ride to school each day. She had missed him when he went away to college. Her mornings were empty and lonely with Joe gone.

Beth sighed and gathered up her tray. Even though Joe had not been around much since leaving for college, Beth still felt as close to him as when they were growing up. The years of separation made no difference in their friendship, though they seldom called each other or wrote. Seeing Joe tonight renewed her feelings for him. She loved him. She always had. She always would.

~4~

*B*eth stepped off the elevator. Dr. Alan Hamilton and a floor nurse conferred just outside the door to Helen's room. At that moment, Beth knew Helen was gone. Dr. Hamilton looked her way and shook his head.

"How long ago?" Beth asked.

"A couple of minutes," Dr. Hamilton answered. "She died peacefully."

"Thanks, Alan, for everything."

"I'm sorry for your loss—for our loss. She volunteered a lot of her time at this hospital."

"She was a second mother to me." Beth stifled a sob and glanced into Helen's room.

Joe sat next to the bed where Helen's lifeless body still lay. The mobile tray beside the bed held sacramental oil and a folded stole. Beth slipped into the room and placed her arm around Joe's shoulders. Helen looked at peace and free from pain. Tears streamed down Beth's cheeks.

"I'm sorry," she said.

Joe acknowledged her presence with a slight nod. He loosened his grip on his mother's hand, placed it lovingly on the bed, then rose and faced Beth.

"We talked for a few minutes," he said, "then she asked me to hear her confession and anoint her."

His voice cracked, but he struggled on. "When I was through, she smiled, closed her eyes, and was gone."

Beth reached up and wiped the tears from his cheeks. Joe gathered her to him and wept. They held each other and cried together, sharing their loss. Joe stepped away from Beth and managed to bring his emotions under control.

"I don't know where to start with making arrangements. I could use your help."

Beth laid her hand on his arm. "Your mother arranged everything weeks ago. I think the best thing for you is to come home with me and get some rest. In the morning we'll go to the funeral home. For now, the hospital will take care of things."

He nodded. "Are you sure I'm not imposing on you?" he asked.

"Not at all. I have the guest room all ready for you."

He took one last look at his mother's still form. "I let her down," he said. "She expected great things of me, and I let her down."

New tears glistened in Beth's eyes, and she squeezed his arm. "You didn't let her down, Joe. She was proud of you and everything you've done. Don't think for a minute you let her down. It's not true."

He smiled a regretful smile. "You and Mom were always my biggest fans and my loudest cheering section. But I never accomplished the one great thing my mother insisted I was destined for."

"How can you be certain? You might have saved the one child that will change the world. You don't know until that child is old enough to make a difference. Look how many boys you've saved from a life of gangs and drugs. You've accomplished great things; you just don't realize it, because all you see are the ones you didn't save."

Beth took his hands in hers and stared at their joined hands. "Your mother shared your letters with me. You've always regretted the kids you couldn't reach. But it's time you rejoice in the ones you have."

Joe shook his head. "Just before she died, Mom insisted I hadn't yet accomplished what God had called me to do. She said she was sorry she wouldn't live to see it."

"If you don't know what you're supposed to do, how can you feel guilty about not accomplishing it? Helen loved you and believed you were destined for greatness. I don't want to diminish what she believed, but all mothers feel the same about their children."

Still holding one of his hands, Beth laid her other hand against Joe's whiskered cheek. "Stop worrying about what you haven't done and be thankful for what you have done. That's what counts, and that's the greatness your mother saw in you."

Joe hugged Beth to him. "You have a knack for making me feel better. You always have." He gently pushed her away and smiled. "Are you always this passionate when you lecture someone?"

Beth blushed. "I just call 'em like I see 'em." She took his hand again and turned toward the door. "Let's go home."

~5~

*J*oe sat at Beth's kitchen table sipping his coffee and staring out the window. *Why did I wait so long to come home?* But he knew the answer. Beth. He'd never been able to purge her from his heart. Because his mother had visited him often in Los Angeles, he hadn't needed to travel home. Distance from Beth kept him focused on what God had planned for him. But seeing Beth again had muddled his priorities. *God, give me strength.*

"Beautiful morning, isn't it?" Beth had slipped into the kitchen unnoticed. She selected a mug from the cupboard and poured herself some coffee.

Joe stood at her greeting. "Morning."

She wore a long teal robe that zipped up the front and matching fuzzy slippers. The morning light illuminated her, highlighting her cheeks and softening her features. Every time Joe saw her he experienced the same sensation—the need to hold her; kiss her; love her. As long as he stayed away he could forget. But with her so close . . .

"You look a thousand miles away," she commented as she sat opposite him. Sunshine streamed in the window, bathing the narrow table and half the kitchen in its warmth.

He sank onto his chair and cradled his coffee mug in his hands. "I suppose I am."

"Did you sleep all right?"

"Yes. Thanks." He took a sip of coffee. "I was oblivious to anything until five thirty. I've been awake since then." He smiled at the slight shake of her head. "Five thirty here would be four thirty in California, right?"

"I guess it would." Beth grinned and sipped her coffee.

"I'm used to getting up at four thirty or five to get some prayer and meditation in before the boys are awake. Then it's complete pandemonium until they're all off to school."

"How many boys do you have living with you now?"

"Twelve. The youngest is eleven and the oldest is seventeen. That old Victorian is bulging at the seams. We've got four boys to a room, but they don't complain much. I've built bunk beds for the rooms to conserve space, although the boys don't always stack them. You'd think I was running a private boy's school, not a home for at-risk kids. Meals are total chaos."

Joe smiled at the thought of his boys. They were his focus. They were what God wanted of him. His work wouldn't bring greatness, as his mother believed, but he was doing God's work and changing a few lives. *If only I could do more.*

"Somehow I've got to find a way to create more room," he said. "Right now we've got another six boys coming to an after-school and weekend program we started in January. At least two of those boys should be a permanent part of Father Joe's Asylum, as the kids call the house, but I don't know where to put them."

He leaned back in his chair and savored the rich coffee. "When I get back, we're going to have a group meeting to see what we can do. It's surprising how willing the boys are to make room for one more, but I'm reluctant to crowd them any more than they already are.

"Besides room, money is a problem. There never seems to be enough. Sometimes I wonder how the Church keeps up with all the demands. Besides the Asylum, there are equally needy programs for the elderly, the homeless, and unwed teen mothers."

Beth marveled at how Joe came alive when he started talking about his boys. His gray-green eyes shone with warmth and love. Why could he not see how much good he was doing? Helen had told her Joe worried about those he couldn't help or reach, but he was making a difference in at least twelve boys' lives and had made a difference in many more lives before them.

Each one of the boys who lived with him

came from broken or dysfunctional homes, often the recipients of brutal beatings. Most had mothers who were addicted to drugs or alcohol; some whose mothers prostituted themselves to make a living; and most whose fathers were in prison, dead, or unknown. Many of the older boys Joe rescued from gangs. He reached younger boys before gangs became a choice.

Each boy was shown love and taught that life offered more than gangs, poverty, prison, or death. Joe had been wrong about not achieving greatness. Countless young lives said otherwise.

Joe leaned forward again, resting his arms on the table. "I worry the Church won't see the progress I've made with these kids. I've asked that the program be expanded to make room for more. That would mean buying a dormitory type building and hiring other people to help out, but I haven't gotten very far with my request." He sighed. "Bishop McKenzie doesn't feel the diocese can take on any more at the moment. So we struggle along for now."

He stopped talking and looked at Beth. "I'm sorry. I'm boring you, aren't I? I tend to get carried away when I talk about my kids."

Beth placed her hand over his. "I'm not a bit bored," she assured him. "You come alive when you talk about your work."

He smiled at her. "I know I'm doing what God called me to do. I just wish I could do more."

"You're only one man, Joe. You do what you can. God knows that."

"Thanks. Keep encouraging me. It helps. Particularly when I begin to worry the Church might change its mind about the program." He covered her hand with his free one.

His touch sent shivers through Beth, making her want more. But she knew he couldn't give her more, and she wouldn't ask.

"In the last ten years we've sent six boys off to college," he continued, his fingers absently stroking her hand. "Several others have successfully completed vocational training and are supporting themselves. Some have married and are raising their own children. I'm continually amazed at the way they've turned out."

"That's because you've given them unconditional love and hope. Those two things are priceless. Two things they hadn't known before they met you."

"I try."

"You've succeeded." Beth swallowed a sip of coffee and tightened her hand on Joe's hand beneath hers. "Who's taking care of things while you're gone?" she asked, trying to ignore her feelings.

"Bishop McKenzie insisted a priest be in

residence while I'm away. An older priest volunteered to stay at the house. Unfortunately, Father Barela is in his eighties and doesn't have a great rapport with the kids." Joe frowned. "Jamal, one of our former boys, has agreed to drop in every evening to see how things are going, and we have several women in the church who have volunteered to help with the meals while I'm gone."

"I'm sure everything will be all right."

Beth slipped her hand from between his and rose. She wanted to remain at the table with her hand surrounded by his, but she knew how dangerous that was.

"Why don't I rustle up something for breakfast," she offered. "While I'm doing that, you can give the funeral home a call, and then call your mother's lawyer and make an appointment. The sooner you get both taken care of, the better."

Joe downed his coffee. "You're right," he said.

Beth watched the sadness creep back into his eyes, replacing the brightness evident moments before. She hated being responsible for the change, but it couldn't be helped. With her hand in his, she had yearned for something she could not have. She reminded herself Joe came home to bury his mother and nothing more.

~6~

*J*oe and Beth sat quietly side by side, staring across the valley floor, its vastness interrupted by the towering sandstone monolith in its center. Shades of beige, brown, and rust were dotted by the grays and greens of sage, piñon, and juniper. The stark beauty of the Colorado National Monument provided them a quiet place to seek God's comfort.

The cool March breeze teased the curls of Beth's hair, and she snuggled deeper into her coat.

She missed Helen's ready smile and soft, musical voice, and wished Helen had confided in Beth about her illness. Helen had sold her house and moved into an assisted living facility when she discovered she had cancer. Her only explanation to Joe and Beth for her move was that she was getting too old to take care of the house the way she wanted to. Neither one suspected she suffered from pancreatic cancer until she was hospitalized. She kept her cancer from them, she said, in order to spare them. In less than three months after her initial diagnosis, she died.

With funeral arrangements finalized and the reading of the will behind them, Joe suggested they drive to the Colorado National Monument. Beth handed him the keys to her Tahoe, and Joe drove to his favorite overlook.

They sat in silence at the canyon edge for a while, letting the peace and majesty of nature comfort them. A piñon jay soared on the air currents, its cry floating back to them on a sudden gust.

Joe inhaled the fresh, crisp air and exhaled slowly. "When I come here, I can feel God's presence in the wind and in the shapes He's carved from the sandstone. No sculptor could ever duplicate the unique masterpiece God has created here. In Los Angeles, when the demands and stress overwhelm me, I close my eyes and picture this spot and peace returns to comfort me. Sometimes I wish I could magically transport this to Los Angeles."

"I used to come here after Peter died to find solace." Beth combed her fingers through her hair. "Sometimes it helped. Other times it only made me miss him more. This was our favorite spot. We were married here."

"I'm sorry I never met Peter. He must have been very special."

Beth smiled as tears moistened her eyes. "He was the kindest, gentlest man I've ever known, and it showed in the way he treated his patients, especially the kids. You'd have thought each one of his young patients belonged to him. He should have been a father. He should have had his own children." A tear trickled down her cheek and dried in the cold air.

Joe took Beth's hands and warmed them between his. "And you should have been a mother. I'm sorry you were deprived of that joy."

She shrugged her shoulders. "Some things aren't meant to be. When we decided we were ready to start a family, my doctor discovered a tumor, and before I had time to take a deep breath, I'd had a complete hysterectomy." Her voice caught, and she swallowed the lump forming in her throat. "And with it any hope of having children. We'd started adoption proceedings a few weeks before Peter . . ." Beth wiped the tears from her cheek. "It just wasn't meant to be."

She rested her head on Joe's shoulder and slipped her arm through his. "It's been almost three years since he was found next to his crumpled bicycle at the roadside. I still miss him. They never did find the hit-and-run driver." She bit her lip to fight back the sorrow rising in her throat. "I could have forgiven the person if he'd only stopped to help. But he just kept going. I haven't been able to forgive that."

Her sobs shook her body, and Joe slipped his arm around her. He stroked her hair and held her until she stopped crying. She accepted his handkerchief to blow her nose.

"I don't understand why God would take away someone so young, someone who had so much to offer," she said.

Joe closed his eyes. How many times had he

wondered the same thing when he held a dying child in his arms, the victim of gang violence?

"God doesn't take people away from us," he heard himself saying. "He lends them to us for a while, and they change our lives and make us better for having known them. Then something inexplicable happens. They're taken away before their time, and God grieves along with us. There's no answer to why, only the promise we'll see them again in heaven. It's that promise that gives us hope and joy."

Joe watched as a tentative smile graced Beth's face.

"Thank you. You always know the right thing to say."

"Not always," he admitted. "I've questioned God many times, but He never seems to mind. And when I'm through questioning, I feel at peace, because the answer is always hope."

"Yes," she whispered. "There's always hope."

~7~

*B*eth parked the Tahoe in the driveway. As she exited the vehicle, steady pounding drifted from the backyard. She slipped through the gate to find Joe hammering a board into place on her deck. With the weather unusually warm for early March, he wore sneakers, jeans, and a sweatshirt, its sleeves pushed up to his elbows. Curly, black hair drifted across his forehead grazing the beads of perspiration as he drove another nail into the wood.

Beth's heart fluttered. Gray flecked the dark hair of his temples and his close-trimmed beard and mustache. His angular face and strong jaw gave him his rugged good looks, and his muscular body gave him more the appearance of a handyman than a priest. A regretful smile crept across Beth's face.

Joe had always known his future. When he was twelve he told Beth he was going to be a priest. At that young age he talked about the importance of serving God. Beth had asked him why he was so certain becoming a priest was what he wanted to do, and he told her about his mother's message from God.

Joe was born one month after his father's death. Helen told Joe his father appeared to her in the hospital room a few hours after Joe's birth. At first Helen thought she was dreaming, but her husband assured her she was not. He had returned, in spirit, to give her a message. Rather than naming the child

after him, she was to name their son Joseph
Zechariah. "God has great plans for him," her
husband said. "He will achieve greatness in the eyes
of God and leave his mark on the world. Love him
and raise him to be strong and compassionate.
Encourage him to become a priest. God will take care
of him and show him the way."

At seven, Beth had been fascinated with such
a romantic story. But as she grew older, Joe's
determination to follow his destiny left her with
mixed feelings. She admired his dedication to his
destiny, but his heart belonged only to God, and she
knew he would never love her the way she loved him.

As she watched him pound another nail into
place, she smiled. He never seemed to falter in his
beliefs or his calling, two of the many qualities she
loved about him. Falling in love with Joe was her
misfortune, and yet she neither regretted nor

questioned her feelings.

Joe looked up from his task and smiled. "Home already? Is it that late?" He glanced at a watch he wasn't wearing, then up at the darkening sky. He rose and leaned against the wooden rail surrounding the deck, his hand still clutching the hammer.

"How was your day?" he asked.

Beth stepped onto the deck and laid a stack of books on the wooden rail. "Busy. Two puppet shows and hordes of kids in the library. There must be a storm coming. The kids were noisy and unruly, and I had to constantly remind them they were in a library. The afternoon kids were far worse than the morning kids. I feel like I've been through a war." She rolled her eyes and crossed them. "I hope I don't see another kid for the next two days."

Joe's low chuckle surprised her.

"What?"

He moved to where she stood and brushed her hair away from her face. "You can't fool me. You loved every minute of it. And if you don't see any kids tomorrow you're going to be extremely disappointed." He let his arm drop to her shoulder and rested it there.

Beth's breath caught in her throat. His unexpected touch sent shivers through her. Gray-green eyes stared into her brown ones, and he smiled. "I'm right, aren't I?" he pressed, raising his eyebrows.

Beth closed her eyes and swallowed to calm herself. He was close enough to kiss her, and she ached to feel his lips against hers. She had never forgotten how they felt the one time he kissed her on their only date.

"I'll let you know in the morning, when I have to face another day." Beth's voice shook as she fought against the sensations running amok inside

her.

~*8*~

*B*eth sat on the edge of her bed, fell back, and closed her eyes. Emotional exhaustion flooded over her, and she fought back tears. The last two weeks had been both wonderful and difficult. Dealing with Helen's death was almost as hard as dealing with her own parents' deaths. At least she had been able to say good-bye to Helen. The accident that took her parents from her, like the one that took Peter, left her no opportunity to emotionally sever the ties. Some days she still expected any one of them to walk through the door.

More than anything, she realized she was tired of dealing with loss. And she was tired of burying her feelings where Joe was concerned. But no matter how much she wanted him to know she loved him, the knowledge would only distress him. She could fight another woman for him, but she could not fight his commitment to God and the Church.

Beth rubbed her eyes and sat up. *No use wishing for something that can't be. Just savor the few hours remaining before he returns to Los Angeles and then let him go. Don't complicate his life any more than it already is.* She pushed aside the image of his face so close to hers, his touch when he brushed her hair aside.

As she changed into jeans, an oversized sweatshirt, and tennis shoes, she mused at how comfortable she felt having Joe around. They spent the day following Helen's funeral on Grand Mesa, where snow still blanketed the rock- and pine-covered landscape. Beth tied her shoes and smiled at the memory of the snowball fight that left them laughing, soaked, and chilled to the bone.

When she returned to work the following week, Joe spent his time making repairs around the house and repainting her living room. He even changed the oil in the Tahoe and tuned the engine. On Tuesday night, Joe had taken his mother's place for family story hour, infusing laughter and wide-eyed wonder in both the kids and their parents with his unique brand of storytelling, inherited, it seemed, from his mother. Tears surfaced and emptiness threatened as Beth faced the reality that Joe's leaving meant hours, days, months of loneliness without her best friend.

Forcing herself to set aside her warring emotions, Beth busied herself in the kitchen preparing her famous chicken enchilada casserole. While working on a tossed green salad, she found herself humming. When she set the table, plates and silverware clinked in time as tune and words flowed from her in reckless abandon.

The savory aroma of chicken, green chili, and onion pulled Joe to the kitchen. He stopped at the kitchen door and leaned against the doorframe. Her back to him, Beth slipped the casserole from the oven, her song filling the kitchen. He smiled at her erratic rendition of *Love Will Keep Us Together.* As he listened, he sucked in a breath, realizing he wanted time to stand still. He wanted more than small patches of time with her. The one thing Joe wanted with Beth he would never have. His vows forbade it.

In spite of his mother's death, the last two weeks had been balm to his troubled heart. Like a fresh breeze, Beth lifted his spirits and gave him new energy. Part of him yearned to stay with her and forget about Los Angeles. But he knew he couldn't stay. He had work to do. And troubled boys who needed him. And promises he had made to God.

Beth removed the oven mitts and turned from the stove. The song caught in her throat and died there. Joe, fresh from the shower, grinned as he watched her face redden. He loved catching her off guard, innocence and self-consciousness written on her face.

"Don't stop," he said, his smile broadening. "I was enjoying it."

She grinned. "You shouldn't sneak up on people that way."

"What sneak? I walked into the kitchen just

like normal. You couldn't hear me above all that racket."

"Racket?" She threw the tea towel she had slung over her shoulder at him. "It was better than Toni Tennille herself." Her look challenged him to agree or suffer the consequences.

He raised his hands in self-defense, one holding the towel she had thrown. "No argument here." He winked. "Need some help?"

She turned, slipped the oven mitts on, and picked up the casserole. "Nope," she said and sashayed past him, a twinkle in her eye. "Supper's ready. Let's eat."

~9~

*T*hey lingered over supper, neither one in a hurry to end the evening. Joe helped Beth with the dishes, drying while she washed. The last plate clinked against the others as he placed it in the cupboard. Joe folded and laid the damp dish towel on the counter and leaned against the edge. Beth felt his gaze on her while she rinsed out the sink.

She dried her hands and smiled at him. "Thanks for your help."

"My pleasure."

"You've done so much around here the last few days. I don't know how to thank you."

"No need. It's the least I could do for you." He crossed his arms over his chest. "Actually, you should thank your dad. He's the one who taught me everything he knew about carpentry and mechanics. I think I'm only beginning to pay him back. I also appreciate everything you did for Mom. She loved you like a daughter, you know."

"I know." Beth turned to stand in front of Joe. "Just the same, I would have had to pay someone quite a bit to do what you've done this week. And that deserves some thanks, so I hope this will do until you're better paid."

She laid her hand at the side of his face and kissed his cheek.

Joe pushed away from the counter and

dropped his hands to Beth's waist, closing the small space between them. She leaned her head back and looked at him. His gaze locked with hers. He looked from her eyes to her lips, then dipped his head. Beth closed her eyes and lifted her face toward him. His lips brushed hers, and she opened her mouth a little, anticipating his next move.

He pushed her away. She opened her eyes to see a storm raging in his. His jaw tightened, and he closed his eyes.

"I can't do this," he murmured. "It's wrong."

He stepped away and turned his back. Beth took a deep breath and stared at the floor.

Joe turned to face her. "If I go any further, Beth, I won't be able to stop. And that would be wrong. I'm not free to love you. Not this way. I'm sorry."

Beth clenched her fists at her side and glared

at him. "So am I," she seethed. "Sorry you serve a church that won't allow you to be a man, or feel as a man should." Tears stung her eyes. "Your religion strips you of the love God intended you to feel. Celibacy is man's law, not God's. It's unnatural, and I'll *never* understand it." She fled from the kitchen, tears streaming down her face.

Joe closed his eyes, battling the war raging inside him. He heard her bedroom door slam and flinched. *Father, give me strength, and help Beth understand. Please.*

He didn't regret wanting to kiss her and that bothered him. What hurt was that Beth was right. Church law stripped him of his most natural need—the need not only to love a woman, but, more important, to marry her.

Beth was the one woman who challenged his

commitment to the priesthood. He could have walked away from his commitment the night he fell in love with her. But instead, he fled and entered seminary, never letting her know how he felt until it was too late for both of them. He had committed too many years to the Church and to the kids who still needed him. He had made his choice.

~10~

Joe lay awake for a several hours, trying to make sense of his feelings. The closed curtains left the room black, letting him concentrate on his troubled thoughts without distractions. Or so he thought. When that didn't work, he opened the curtains and slid the window open a couple of inches hoping the fresh air would help him sleep. But sleep refused to enter the room.

With sleep no longer an option, and exhausted

from praying, he rose. Dressed in his jeans and a T-shirt, his stockinged feet cushioning his footsteps, he slipped from his room and into the living room. The picture window curtains were open, and the streetlight cast eerie shadows across the lawn and into the room. He stopped behind the couch that separated the living room from the dining area and stared out into the moonless night.

Resting his hands on the back of the couch, he closed his eyes and wondered how he could smooth things over with Beth. He didn't want to leave with so much anger between them. As he opened his eyes, a movement from the corner chair caught his attention. He stiffened as Beth moved to stand beside him. Neither spoke for a few moments.

"I'm sorry for my tirade earlier," Beth said barely above a whisper. "I was out of line."

She wore a flannel nightshirt and slippers, and

her hair was ruffled as though she had tossed and turned for a while before getting up. She combed a few curls away from her face, then clasped her hands behind her.

"You don't have to apologize, Beth. I was the one out of line. You offered me a simple kiss of appreciation, and for a moment I wanted it to be more. I'm sorry."

"You're too generous, Joe, giving me an out like that." She cleared her throat. "The truth is, I kissed you hoping you'd react exactly as you did. And if you hadn't, I would have placed the next kiss on your lips."

Joe frowned at her. In the silence that followed Beth's revelation, he studied her face. She stared straight ahead, licked her lips, and closed her eyes. Joe felt the war raging inside her; the same war raging inside him.

"I wanted to seduce you," she said. "I'm not proud of it, but it's true." She sighed and turned toward him. "Joe, I'm in love with you. I've been in love with you since I was six. And most of my life I've known my love would be one-sided." Beth's voice caught. "But tonight, I wanted *you* to love *me*." A tear trickled down her cheek.

He gazed out the window, unsure how to respond to her confession. "What about Peter?" he asked.

She smiled. "I fell in love with him because he was so much like you, and you weren't available. I could have been happy the rest of my life with Peter if . . ."

Beth bit her lip. "I don't feel guilty about loving you. There's nothing wrong with it. God made man and woman to complement and complete each other. But my Protestant upbringing makes it difficult for me to understand why a church would put such stringent controls on a man. It's not natural."

She hesitated, and Joe searched for something to say. The furnace fan clicked on and warm air filled the room.

"Your church encourages marriage," Beth continued, "for everyone except its priests. For them it's wrong. Marriage is not wrong. It's a lifetime commitment between a man and a woman bound by love and respect. I would think being married would help you deal with the pressures of ministering to others. You'd have someone to trust, to confide in."

Joe shoved his hands in his back pockets and took a deep breath. "By not marrying, I'm unencumbered by the demands of another person for my time and my emotions. God is my confidant. All my energy goes to His work. I've pledged to remain unmarried in order to serve God."

"Do you love me, Joe?"

He knew her question was a simple need for the truth without expectations.

"So much it hurts." He turned toward her and grasped her shoulders, hoping, praying he could find the words to make her understand. "I wish I had the freedom to marry you, Beth, but I don't. I took a vow, and unless God Himself tells me otherwise, I will remain unmarried. I have no other choice."

"There's always a choice," she whispered.

He dropped his hands from her shoulders, needing to put some small token of distance between them. "You're not making this easy for me."

"I'm not trying to. I'm fighting as hard for what I believe in as you are. My faith sees the love between a man and a woman as a beautiful thing for everyone, including our ministers. It doesn't saddle us with unreasonable laws."

He turned toward the window and stared out at nothing. The clock on the wall ticked out a steady rhythm. "Sometimes," he said, "I envy you your beautiful and uncomplicated faith. But I can't abandon my own on a whim."

"I know that."

Silence crowded into the room, an unwelcome visitor wedged between them. Seconds—a lifetime—crept by.

Still staring out the window, Joe snarled, "*What* do You want me to *do*, God?"

Beth flinched at Joe's outburst. The glow from the streetlight highlighted the anger and frustration on his face. She wondered if he had forgotten she was there. Her own anger subsided as she watched him struggle with his. Fresh tears stung her eyes.

"Since last fall, Lord, You have turned my life

upside down," he accused. "And just when I think some peace has come into it, You turn it upside down again. I've prayed for guidance, but Your silence is deafening. Father, what do You *want* from me?"

~11~

*T*he pain of Joe's questions and the distress in his voice moved Beth to action. She slipped behind him, circled her arms around Joe's waist, and rested her head on his back.

"I'm so sorry," she whispered, hoping to comfort him.

He turned in her arms and held her to him, letting his cheek rest against her head. He clutched her so tight she could barely breathe. After a few minutes he loosened his hold, pushed away from her, and leaned against the back of the couch. He took her hands in his.

He stared at their hands as he spoke. "Last October I attended a lecture at St. John's Seminary given by Father Lucas Ramirez. He's best known for his recent and somewhat controversial book about the Church and the second millennium. He's also written numerous commentaries about the New and Old Testaments. I own all of them.

"That night he spoke about Christ's life, and I remember feeling rejuvenated and inspired when the lecture was over. Father Ramirez was a powerful speaker, and I wanted a chance to talk to him for a few minutes after the lecture, so I waited until everyone had gone."

Joe took a deep breath. "When I walked up to him I offered him my hand and started to tell him how much I enjoyed his lecture, but I only got two words out."

Joe squeezed Beth's hands. "As he clutched my hand in both of his, he smiled and said, 'This is truly a blessing. You are indeed *the* man of God, and He has honored me with your presence.' I was speechless. I didn't know what to say. I wasn't wearing my collar or anything that would tell him I was a priest. He just knew.

"I know my mouth was open, but no words came out. Father Ramirez put a hand at my back, ushering me out the door as he did. 'God has many changes in store for you, my son,' he said. 'You will be faced with difficult choices, but trust in God. He *will* show you the way.'

"I finally found my voice and blurted, 'I don't understand.' Father Ramirez stopped walking and smiled. 'You will,' he said. 'Remember, the Church, any church, isn't always right. Churches are run by men. Listen to God. You'll know His voice when you hear it.'

"He walked away, and I called after him, 'please explain.' But he waved me off, saying he was late for another engagement." Joe closed his eyes and waited for what seemed to Beth an eternity. "His last words as he left the building were, 'Trust God and let love be your strength.'

"I don't know how long I stood in the empty hallway staring after him. When I did move, I began to wonder if I had imagined the whole conversation. But I know it was real."

Joe shifted, but still clutched Beth's hands. She held her breath, hoping he would continue, and sighed in relief when he did.

"The next week, Bishop McKenzie called me into his office and informed me he was adding a homeless shelter to my duties. I'm required to spend part of my time at the shelter. I know the homeless need ministering to, but the added duties take me away from the kids at home, and I have less time to talk to the gangs. I'd gotten a pretty good dialogue going with a couple of the gangs, but now that time has been cut short."

He shook his head. "On top of that, a month ago, I was informed our funds for the Asylum were being cut, and I would have to let our housekeeper go. Several women from the church have volunteered a few hours of their time each week, but it doesn't begin to make up for what we lost.

"Then I got word about Mom. I was only going to come for a few days, but Bishop McKenzie insisted I take two weeks. He stressed I needed time away. I reluctantly agreed, knowing full well I had no intention of staying the entire two weeks.

"I intended to return to Los Angeles right after the funeral, but I found myself wanting to spend time with you." He cupped Beth's chin with his hand, and she held her breath. "And that's when I realized how much I still love you."

~12~

*J*oe pushed away from the couch and grasped Beth's shoulders. "Do you know when I fell in love with you?"

She shook her head, unable to speak. She had not known until a few moments ago he loved her at all. She always believed her feelings were one-sided. She saw his devotion to God and the Church as his only love.

"I fell in love with you the night I took you to

your senior prom. Do you remember that night?"

She smiled and nodded. How could she forget? Joe had come home to visit a few days before he entered seminary. Beth promised she would show off her new dress to Helen and Joe before her date arrived. But a few minutes before she was to go next door, Beth's date called. He was sick with the flu and could not take her to the prom. Heartsick, she fled upstairs to her room, crying out her disappointment.

Thirty minutes later, Beth's mother knocked on her door to tell Beth her date had arrived. When Beth entered the living room, her hair and makeup freshly done, there stood Joe, dressed in a suit and holding a corsage box. She found out later Joe and Helen decided Beth shouldn't miss her senior prom. Joe contacted Beth's date, picked up the corsage and boutonniere, and arrived at her house as her date. Beth's love for Joe had grown tenfold that night.

"When you walked into the living room," Joe said, "in that strapless blue dress, your hair piled up in soft curls on your head, and a look of wonder on your face, I thought my heart would burst. I was amazed by the beautiful young woman who stood before me. And when I kissed you good night, I knew I was lost. I knew I loved you, and that simple thought scared me.

"All my life I'd prepared myself for the priesthood and to dedicate my life to the Church. Funny how life can blindside priorities. One date with you, and I was questioning my decision. I didn't sleep that night, struggling with what I had discovered. The next morning Mom couldn't stop talking about how excited I must be about entering seminary the next week. My decision came down to the simple fact I couldn't disappoint her, or God." He closed his eyes for a moment.

"I walked away from my feelings then," he said and looked at Beth, "and I have to now." He tightened his grip on her shoulders.

"But you don't," she said.

"Beth, I can't walk away from my life's work. I can't walk away from my boys."

"I'm not asking you to walk away from them, Joe. I accept your commitment to them and the Church. I have no choice. All I'm asking for is one night. I can be content with that." She grasped his arms. "One night only you and I and God know about."

Joe cradled her face in his hands, his gaze penetrating hers. "I've taught the boys the importance of commitment and marriage. I've taught them that to make love to a woman and not marry her is wrong."

"But this is not wrong, Joe," she argued. "We

love each other, and the only thing that's keeping us from a marriage commitment is your church's antiquated laws." Tears trickled onto her cheeks, and she looked away. "I'm sorry. That was unfair."

He gathered her against him. "There's a great deal of truth in what you say, which only makes this harder."

She raised her head to look at him and touched his lips with her fingers. His hand at the back of her head drew her toward him. She lifted her mouth to his, and what little resistance remained died when their lips touched. His mouth claimed hers in a long and passionate kiss.

When their lips parted, he looked into her eyes, searching for answers and finding only love.

"What's happening to me, Beth?" he asked, his voice a hoarse whisper. "Is this my destiny? Does my future lie with you, or am I being tested? Why can't I see anything but your face when I close my eyes, no matter how hard I pray?"

"I can't answer your questions, Joe. I'm sorry. All I know is I love you, and this feels right."

His mouth crushed hers. The years of loving, needing, wanting, faded away as they surrendered to the fire building between them.

~*13*~

*J*oe stood on the deck, the morning sun bathing him in warmth. Birds welcomed the new day with their song, and the first hint of spring lingered in the air. In his morning prayers, Joe had struggled with the guilt of his actions. And yet, for the first time in his life, he felt complete. Not that God and His work had not fulfilled him, but there always seemed a void in his heart. Now he knew what the void was.

He thought about the words of St. Paul. *It is*

*good for (a man) to stay unmarried . . . But if they
cannot control themselves, they should marry, for it is
better to marry than to burn with passion.*

Joe knew what he felt for Beth was more than
a burning passion. She had been right. They
complemented and completed each other. They gave
each other strength and comfort. In another lifetime
they would have married and raised a family. In this
lifetime they were denied the best of what God
designed for a man and a woman.

A sense of loss washed over Joe. Because of
what had passed between him and Beth, everything,
yet nothing, had changed. The love they shared could
no longer be denied. Love brought them together, and
now commitment demanded they part.

Joe gripped the deck's top rail and closed his
eyes. He raised his face to the morning sun and
basked in its warmth.

God, give me the strength to walk away without destroying the love between us. Help Beth understand the depth of my commitment to You, my boys, and my church. Guide me back to the path You have chosen for me. And forgive me my sin.

Beth watched Joe from the kitchen. Her heart ached for him and his struggle. She had lied to him about one night being enough. One night wasn't enough. She wanted a lifetime with him. A lifetime she knew she could never have. He claimed he wasn't free to love her. But he was wrong. He was free to love her; he wasn't free to marry her.

When Joe entered the kitchen, Beth poured two mugs of coffee and handed one to him.

"Just the way you like it," she smiled. "Hot and black."

Joe returned her smile. "Thanks."

Beth leaned against the counter. "What would you like for breakfast?"

"Nothing right now. I'll fix myself something after you've gone to work."

"I'm not going to work today."

His eyes narrowed.

"Don't frown at me," she admonished. "I'm just not up to going to work today. I want, no, *need* to spend the day with you."

Joe set his coffee on the counter and cradled her face in his hands. He searched her eyes, and she fought the tears rushing to surface.

"Beth, I have to return to Los Angeles. I have to continue with my work. You said one ni—"

"I know what I said." She moved away from him and swiped at a tear escaping down her cheek.

Joe pulled Beth to him and gathered her into his arms. She fought back a sob and whispered a quick prayer for strength.

"One night was not enough for me either," he said, "but we have no other choice. I can't denounce my priesthood and walk away from those kids. Even if another priest took my place, it would take him too long to establish a rapport with the kids and the gangs. The church would lose the ground we've fought so hard to gain. We can't wait that long for a chance to rescue even one kid, or take a chance on losing the ones we've already reached. I *have* to go back."

Beth fought for composure. "What if you found funding through other sources? You could still do what you're doing, and we could be together."

Joe held her at arms' length. "I understand your hope, but even if I could find funding, it would take years to establish enough money to match what the Church is providing now. Hundreds of organizations plea for money and are turned down, or funded with a fraction of what they need."

Beth looked away and lowered her head, knowing what Joe said was true; wishing it were not.

"What would the kids who are living with me do until I secured the money I needed? The majority of them would either return to gang life, or they would lose the self-confidence and hope they've gained and return to a life on the streets."

"I could get a job and help."

"I appreciate your offer, but it wouldn't be enough." Joe placed his hand under Beth's chin and lifted her head, forcing her to look at him. "I love these kids, and I can't let them down. As much as I love you, I won't abandon them. If you could meet them, see what's been accomplished, you'd understand."

Beth touched his cheek and smiled. Because

she loved him, her next words were the most difficult ones she had ever spoken.

"I know you love me," she said, "but I also know how much you love those kids. I won't ask you to abandon them. Ever. But I won't stop loving you, and I'll always be here if you need me."

Beth saw the gratitude reflected in Joe's eyes. He gathered her in his arms and whispered, "Thank you."

She had done the only thing she could under the circumstances.

~14~

$\mathcal{A}$s the taxi carrying Joe to the airport pulled away from her home, Beth's tears flowed like a rampaging flood. She felt she was in mourning again. She experienced the euphoria of Joe declaring his love for her, and then the pain of knowing she could never be his wife.

Days stretched into weeks, and with each new day, Beth accepted, little by little, life without Joe. She was never more thankful for her job than she was at this time in her life. Story hours, puppet shows, helping children and parents find books, and planning the summer reading program kept her days filled, and thoughts of Joe at bay. Only at night did she have time to miss him. Only at night did she pray God would find a way for them to be together.

By mid-April, Beth's life had returned to normal, at least as normal as possible under the circumstances. But she lacked her usual enthusiasm and energy, and for more mornings than she cared to admit, she fought a queasy stomach. She confided her feelings to her friend and fellow librarian one morning over coffee.

"Either I have the longest lasting flu bug ever, or something else is wrong. Maybe I just need some mega vitamins."

Her friend laughed. "If I didn't know better, I'd think you were pregnant. That's exactly how I felt in the beginning with all four of my kids."

Beth chuckled. "We both know that's impossible."

"I suggest you make an appointment with your doctor to be sure nothing serious is going on."

"I suppose you're right. No sense putting it off. Besides, I'm sick and tired of going without breakfast."

The light gray walls of Dr. Alan Hamilton's office did little to help Beth feel better. She stared at a photograph above his desk of snow-capped mountains towering over a glass-smooth lake and imagined herself gliding across the water in a canoe. The peaceful image failed to calm her nerves as she waited to hear the results of her exam. Alan had chided her for not coming in sooner and for going two months past her yearly physical. She had been so wrapped up in taking care of Helen she forgot to make her annual appointment.

Beth squirmed. What was taking Alan so long? He stepped into his office, startling her. The frown on his face triggered a stab of fear in her. She took a deep breath and waited for him to speak.

He looked at her and shook his head. Leaning forward, he rested his arms on his desk.

"I was in the operating room as attending physician when Dr. Elliott did your hysterectomy. I watched every move he made. His surgery was flawless and everything that needed to be removed was. He was very thorough."

Apprehension surfaced with a vengeance. She hadn't been this frightened since she was diagnosed with uterine cancer. After the surgery and months of follow-up treatment, she was given a clean bill of health. Now Alan, her deceased husband's colleague and best friend, was about to tell her the cancer had returned.

"Just give me the bad news, Alan. Don't sugarcoat it. I can handle it." Her words sounded braver than she felt.

Alan shook his head. "I'm not altogether sure it's bad news. Impossible news, maybe. Unbelievable, actually." He took Beth's hand. "As far as I can determine, you're pregnant."

The color drained from Beth's face, and she stared open-mouthed at him.

"It sounds crazy, but everything indicates you're going to be a mother. I've seen what I believed were miracles before, but this one is the granddaddy of them all."

He sat back in his chair. "I've made arrangements for you to have some tests done at the hospital today. The lab will send me the results as soon as the tests are completed. I want you back here by four this afternoon. We have a lot to discuss if my diagnosis is correct."

Beth's voice wavered as she verbalized the thoughts running through her head. "This is impossible, Alan. There's no way—"

"I assume you've been seeing someone."

"No. Yes. Helen's son, Joe. But that was weeks ago." Beth's face reddened. Her relationship with Joe was private, yet her doctor needed to know.

"Isn't he a priest?"

"Yes."

"Then the two of you are going to have some serious decisions to make."

"If I tell him," she whispered. She could not possibly be pregnant. It was a complication she hadn't even considered. "Are you sure, Alan?"

"With any other pregnancy, I'd stake my

reputation on it. But in this case, let's wait for the results from the hospital tests."

Beth sat in her car staring at the parking lot by Alan's office. A young mother pushed a stroller toward the building with one hand, pulling a tow-headed little boy with the other. Beth had often imagined herself as that mother before cancer had robbed her of the dream. She shook her head slowly, wondering if she could, or should, hope Alan was right. And if he was, what would she do?

~15~

*B*eth sat on the couch in the hospital lobby and stared at the green, ivory, and gold mosaic tile pattern on the opposite wall. The shock of Alan's diagnosis still lingered, and only minutes ago, the lab technician had congratulated her on her pregnancy. Absorbed with the enormity of her situation, she didn't notice the old man standing near her until he spoke.

"You're looking a bit peaked young lady. Are

you okay?"

She tried to ignore him, but he persisted.

"Name's Gabe," he said and offered her his hand.

Uneasy, she tightened her grip on her purse, ready to leave, when she glanced at his face. Something about him made her want to confide in him. Perhaps it was his clear blue eyes, or the genuine concern that invited her to speak candidly to a stranger.

She clasped his hand. "I don't know if I'm okay," she said in answer to his question. A tear slithered down her cheek.

Gabe sat beside her and put his arm around her. "There, there." He patted her shoulder. "Everything will be all right. Now, what's troubling you?"

Beth wiped her eyes with a Kleenex she dug

out of her purse. "I'm pregnant. It's impossible, but I am."

"Pregnant? Now that's something to be happy about, not sad. Why, a baby is God's greatest miracle."

She smiled at his enthusiasm. "Normally, I'd feel the same way, but this baby tends to complicate things."

He raised his free hand as if to stop something. "No, don't tell me. You're not married and the father of the baby isn't free to marry you. Am I right?"

Beth stared at him. "How did you know?"

"Oldest story in the book," he said. "But in your case, I don't think it's as complicated as you might think."

Before Beth could question how he knew about "her case," he continued. "You have to look at this baby as a gift from God. And God *never* bestows a gift He doesn't intend to bring blessings far greater than you would expect."

Gabe took Beth's hand and squeezed it. Looking into her eyes, he said, "Don't be afraid, Beth. You're very special to God, and He *will* take care of you. Remember, nothing is impossible with God. Just have faith."

He smiled and rose. "God is in the business of miracles, and this is one of His greatest. Trust Him."

As he walked away, Beth realized he had referred to her by name. "Wait," she called as he disappeared around a corner. She ran after him, but when she turned the same corner, he was gone.

"How did you know my name?" she whispered to the empty corridor.

His words replayed in her mind. *Don't be afraid. You're very special to God. God is in the business of miracles.* And then she smiled. Gabe was right. Trusting God was the only answer.

"Okay, God," she said aloud. "Show me what to do."

~16~

*O*n the return trip to Alan's office, Beth thought about Joe and how he would react to the news she was pregnant. She knew he would not only offer to marry her, he would insist on it. She also knew marrying her meant he would no longer be welcome in the Church as a priest. And that meant giving up the Asylum and the boys he loved as his own. Growing inside her was the one thing that would give her what she always wanted, but at what cost to Joe?

While she waited for Alan to finish with his last patient, Beth mulled over her options. When Alan finally ushered her into his office, she knew the only course of action open to her. As she sat opposite Alan and waited for him to read through the test results, a quiet peace settled on her, and she smiled.

Alan set the tests on his desk and sat back in his chair. With his elbows resting on the chair arms, he steepled his hands together and studied Beth a moment. He shook his head, and a smile spread across his face.

"It's a miracle. That's the only word for it. Nothing like this has ever happened, to my knowledge. I have no scientific explanation for what's happened. Somehow, your body has regenerated ovaries and a uterus. In eight months, give or take a day or two, you're going to be a mother."

"I know." Beth bit her bottom lip and looked away, fighting back joyful tears threatening to surface.

Alan studied her a moment. "You are planning on keeping this baby, aren't you?"

Beth's gaze locked on his. "Of course I'm going to keep the baby. How could you think I'd consider otherwise?"

"Sorry, but you looked a little uncertain. You aren't married, and the father is a priest."

"This child *is* a miracle, Alan, as you pointed out. And I do intend to keep it. Nothing or no one can take this baby away from me, except God."

"The father has every right to know."

"I know that. And I'll tell him. But I prefer to wait until I've gotten through the third month. Then I'll tell him."

Beth shifted in her chair. "Look, Alan, I can't

ask him to give up his life's work just to marry me. I'm not sure what will happen. But I have decided to take a leave of absence from the library before I start showing. After the baby is born, I'll probably go back to work. Peter made some sound investments before he . . . I can afford to be away from work for a while."

"This isn't going to be easy for you. Even if the father decides to leave the priesthood and marry you, there will be difficulties."

"I know that, too. But God has blessed me with a child I never thought I'd have. Whatever the difficulties, He *will* see me through them." She smiled.

"Then you and I will have to help Him out by taking the best care of you and this baby we possibly can." Alan picked up a prescription pad. "I'm going to write out a prescription for some vitamins, and I want you to watch what you eat. No junk food. No caffeine. No alcohol. Lots of fruits and vegetables. I have some pamphlets outlining both a healthy diet and exercise." He tore the prescription he had written from the pad and handed it to Beth. "Healthy food, exercise, and plenty of rest. Let's not take any chances with this baby."

"I intend to take excellent care of both of us."

Alan walked Beth to the waiting room. From behind the receptionist's desk he gathered up several pamphlets and handed them to her. "My receptionist is gone for the day, so call tomorrow and make an appointment for a month from today. But don't hesitate to call me if you have any problems, no matter how minor they might seem."

He took Beth's hand and squeezed it. "And if you need any moral support, day or night, call."

"Thanks, Alan, I will." Beth kissed him on the cheek. "I'll see you in a month."

~*17*~

*T*he insistent beeping intruded on Joe's meditation. He flipped off the alarm, sighed, and crossed himself, wincing as he rose from beside the bed. Three hours on his knees left his legs numb, and he gripped the dresser beside his bed to steady himself. Feeling crept into his legs, tingling and burning as the blood flowed through his veins.

He lifted his open Bible from the bed and read aloud the highlighted text from Psalm 51.

"Have mercy on me, O God, according to your unfailing love; according to your great compassion blot out my transgressions. Wash away all my iniquity and cleanse me from my sin . . . . Create in me a pure heart, O God, and renew a steadfast spirit within me. Do not cast me from your presence or take your Holy Spirit from me. Restore to me the joy of your salvation and grant me a willing spirit, to sustain me."

Making the sign of the cross, he whispered, "Amen."

In thirty minutes the household would explode with grumbling, laughter, and arguments as the boys vied for one of the two bathrooms and scurried to dress for school. Joe loved the morning chaos at the Asylum, at least until the last month. But each morning became a little harder for him than the last. Lack of sleep from restless nights and hours of prayer each night and every morning left him exhausted.

Since he had returned from Colorado, the added weight of his guilt over Beth left him questioning his fitness as a priest and an example to already troubled boys. He had been tested, not by God, but by his own weakness, and he had failed. No amount of penance eased his troubled conscience. Five days of fasting and hours on his knees failed to salve his guilt and relieve his thoughts of Beth.

Over and over he questioned why he had given in to his physical needs and his feelings for Beth. He allowed himself to become complacent about his commitment to God while he was in Colorado. Beth had been a temptation for years; one he managed to handle each time he saw her, but this time he let his defenses down. In the process, he hurt Beth and failed God.

His confession to Father Barela, a retired

priest he admired and respected, had been an attempt to right himself with God.

Father Barela had welcomed Joe into his small apartment. The sparsely furnished two-room apartment accommodated a crowded floor-to-ceiling bookcase the length of one wall, the only evidence of extravagance. Father Barela did not own a television or any of the modern amenities evident in most homes.

"Please sit down, Father Joe." Father Barela gestured to a straight-backed wooden chair. "To what do I owe the pleasure of this visit?"

Instead of sitting, Joe knelt before Father Barela. "Bless me Father, for I have sinned. I have committed adultery as surely as if I were married. I have been with a woman—a woman I love, but that is no excuse. Fifteen years ago I denied my feelings for her in order to serve God. And now I have broken my vow to Him."

Father Barela placed his hand on Joe's shoulder. "You are obviously carrying a great burden to come to me like this. Why don't you sit down, and we'll talk about this sin you have committed."

"Thank you, Father." Joe rose and sat in the chair Father Barela indicated earlier.

"You are seeking God's forgiveness, yet I think you have doubts, even though you know in your heart God has forgiven you." Father Barela smiled and waited for Joe to respond.

"I know God forgives. I'm having difficulty forgiving myself. And sometimes I wonder if I should give up my priesthood. In quiet moments I think of her. When I close my eyes I see her smile and the sparkle in her eyes. And when I sleep, I dream of her."

"Do you want to marry her? Do you love her

enough to give up your ministry?"

"Sometimes I think I do. Then I think of my work in the Church and my boys, and I know I am doing God's will. Yet I long for her."

Father Barela raised an eyebrow. "Is this longing perhaps only a need for physical release?"

Joe leaned forward and rested his arms on his knees. Staring at the floor, he answered, "No. I long for her in all ways. She's understanding, supportive, and makes me feel whole. I can talk to her about anything. She's made no demands on me. She understands and accepts my dedication to the Church."

Joe raised his head, pleading and uncertainty clouding his eyes. "Why does the Church deny us the joy of marriage and family, when those two things are so important to God?"

"Remember Father, we are married to the

Church, just as Christ is. The parishioners are our family. Our vow of celibacy leaves us unencumbered in order to serve God."

"Our vows leave us empty!" Joe clenched his fists and leaned back in his chair.

"You are troubled because of your feelings for a woman. She is tangible; God is spirit. It is God you should be seeking. Fast for five days and spend as much time as possible in prayer. If you can't sleep, pray. If thoughts of her intrude on your day, pray. Open your heart and mind to God's council. Seek God's will, and He will prove faithful."

Father Barela stood and laid his hands on Joe. "Our Lord Jesus Christ taught us God is a forgiving God. 'For if you forgive other people when they sin against you, your heavenly Father will also forgive you.' And Paul, in his letter to the Ephesians wrote, 'In Him we have redemption through His blood, the forgiveness of sins, in accordance with the riches of God's grace.' You have confessed your sin. Go and sin no more."

Joe had followed Father Barela's advice, but he found no answers. He accepted that God had forgiven him for his one night with Beth, but he couldn't forgive himself. And he couldn't stop loving or wanting her no matter how hard he prayed.

He struggled through his days, his concentration on even simple tasks difficult at best. Once he found himself on the other side of town from his intended destination, with no recollection of how he had arrived there. The Asylum and the homeless shelter both suffered from Joe's personal struggle. He lacked the discipline to come to terms with his feelings for Beth and the strength to put those feelings aside.

"How could I ignore years of dedication to

God—throw it all away in just one night?" he asked himself over and over. But it wasn't one night. It was a lifetime of loving Beth and loving the Church and having to choose between the two.

As the stinging spray of the shower pounded life back into Joe, he forced everything from his mind and concentrated on the day ahead. Javier needed extra attention with his English lessons. Joe had put Javier off for nearly two weeks, something he had never done with any of his boys before. Yet Frankie, their newest resident, worried him the most. The last few days, Frankie showed signs of distress, and Joe could no longer ignore the problem.

"God, help me," he whispered as he turned off the spray and reached for a towel. *If only I could see Beth again. If only I could be sure she doesn't resent me for walking away. If only I could rid myself of this guilt over hurting her. If only I could forgive myself for betraying You and the Church. If only . . .*

Joe shook his head to banish his troubled thoughts. While he dressed he realized what he needed most was complete forgiveness. Not just forgiveness from God, but forgiveness from Beth. Yet how could he ask Beth to forgive him when he could not forgive himself?

All the hours he spent in penance and prayer hadn't answered the one question he kept asking himself. Did he love Beth more than his promise to God and his commitment to the Church? And the only answer he received was he could not abandon his boys.

As he entered the kitchen, Moises turned from the refrigerator, holding a half-full milk jug.

"Hey, Pops, you forgot to get milk. You want me to run get some?"

Joe groaned. He should have picked up

several gallons of milk on his way home from the shelter the night before. He had forgotten.

"No, Moises. I'll go. You get breakfast started."

Joe grabbed the van keys and promised himself on the way out the door he would set his personal troubles aside and concentrate on what God had called him to do.

~18~

*B*eth approached the door marked "Carol Murphy, Library Director" with trepidation. Was her position in jeopardy? The voters had turned down a mill levy increase, and rumor had it some positions would have to be cut. Before she could knock, the door opened.

"Thanks for coming so quickly, Beth." Carol motioned her inside. "Please, sit down. I have some good news."

Beth settled in a chair across from the director's desk.

Carol continued talking as she sat in her chair. "As you're well aware, our summer reading program from last year was submitted to the American Library Association for consideration of their *Excellence in Library Programming Award*. I've just received word our library has won the award for this year."

Beth was stunned. The same summer reading game had taken first place at the state level. She never expected it to win in a national competition. Libraries in much larger cities most often received the prestigious award.

"We are to receive the plaque and recognition in two weeks at the annual convention in Los Angeles. I can't get away, so we want you to represent the library at the ceremonies on Friday night. After all, who better to receive the award than the person who gave birth to the idea and then gave it substance?"

"I had a lot of help."

"It was successful because of your leadership. It's appropriate you accept the award."

"Thank you, Carol."

"Get with our travel agent and make the arrangements." Carol handed Beth a folder. "This contains location, dates, and other pertinent information. Enjoy the time away. You've looked like you needed it lately. I know Helen Connor's death was hard on you."

Tears welled in Beth's eyes. "She was a second mother to me. I miss her terribly." Helen's absence in her life still weighed heavily on Beth. She wiped an errant tear and rose to leave. "Thanks for the opportunity to accept the award. It means more to me than you realize."

Carol smiled. "You're welcome."

Beth sat in her office and stared at the folder the director had given her. Her boss had no idea the gift she'd given Beth. Joe wanted her to visit Los Angeles and see firsthand the work he was doing, and she had just been handed the means to do it. All she needed was her doctor's okay.

Two days before she was scheduled to leave for Los Angeles, Beth called Joe. She could hear the smile in his voice when she told him she would be seeing him in a few days.

"I can hardly wait," he said. "I've missed you."

"I've missed you, too."

"I can't wait for you to meet the boys. You'll be able to see why my work means so much to me, Beth. I need you to understand and accept the choice

I've made."

"I'm looking forward to it, Joe. I'll call as soon as I get to Los Angeles and get settled into the hotel. By then I'll have a finalized schedule for the convention, and we can figure out when to get together."

"Good. I'll see you in a few days, then."

Beth fidgeted on the black leather couch of the hotel lobby. Positioned so she could see the front entrance, she felt like a teenager waiting for her first date to arrive. Several times she glanced at the ornate ceiling, marveling at the artwork. Whenever someone entered, her heart raced. She glanced at her watch and bit her lower lip. Joe was thirty minutes late. Had she misunderstood him?

She rose to find a telephone, when a tall, muscular young black man approached her. His dreadlocks, baggy clothes, and rhythmic swagger to his step were in themselves not threatening, but the way he kept glancing around him left Beth uneasy. Her heart jumped to her throat when he spoke her name.

"Mrs. Stevens?" he asked.

She looked to see if any hotel employee might be close by if she needed help.

"I'm sorry to bother you, ma'am, but are you Mrs. Stevens?"

"Y-yes," she answered.

He grinned. "I thought so. Father Joe described you perfectly. My name's Jamal." He offered his hand. When Beth didn't take it, he let it drop to his side. "I've come to pick you up. I'm afraid Father Joe has been detained and can't come himself."

"Oh." Joe had mentioned a Jamal in his letters to Helen, but she was uncertain this young man was the same Jamal. His eyes and smile implied trust, but Beth was in unfamiliar territory. She decided caution was warranted.

"I appreciate you coming to get me, but if you don't mind, I'll wait until Father Joe can come himself."

Beth expected Jamal to take offense at her refusal, and she prepared to defend her position.

His smile only got bigger. "I don't blame you. You're smart not to trust a stranger. Especially a black one in a white neighborhood," he added and winked. "Father Joe figured you might be reluctant to go with me, so he told me to tell you that you're as safe with me as you were with him when he sent Billy Adams packin' a long time ago."

Beth stared. "He told you about Billy Adams?"

"Yep. Like most bullies, he didn't stick around

when confronted." Jamal scratched his head and frowned. "Let's see now, you were a first grader, Billy was in the fourth grade, and Father Joe was in sixth grade." The grin spread across his face. "Did I get it right?"

Beth smiled and offered Jamal her hand. "It's very nice to meet you Jamal," she said as she shook hands with him. "Where are you parked?"

Once she was settled in a van with "Father Joe's Asylum" printed on the side, Beth relaxed. "How far is the Asylum?" she asked.

Jamal frowned. "Ummm, we're not going directly to the house. We're going to the hospital. Father Joe's there."

~19~

*F*ear stabbed Beth's heart, and she felt the color drain from her face. "The hospital?"

Jamal glanced at her and grimaced. "Now I've gone and done it. Nothin' to worry 'bout, ma'am. Honest. He's gonna be all right. It's a superficial cut. Didn't catch anything vital and—"

"'*Cut*?'" Alarm pierced Beth's heart and surfaced through her voice. "What do you mean 'cut?'"

Jamal slammed his hand against the steering wheel and uttered an unintelligible oath under his breath. Beth jumped.

"Man, I'm sorry." He shook his head. "My bedside manner is usually much better than this. I should have eased you into this. Those of us who grew up on the streets have seen so much violence that this seems a minor incident. But you're not from here, and I apologize."

The van screeched to a halt at a red light. "Father Joe is waiting to get stitched up, but the cut is not life threatening, so you don't need to worry. He's fine."

Beth managed to calm her racing heart. "Tell me what happened. I'll take your word for it that he's going to be all right." She tried to smile.

Jamal eased the van forward as the light turned green

"Frankie, one of Father Joe's boys, broke the rules and went back to his old neighborhood to try to talk a friend out of joining a gang. When Pops—Father Joe—found out, he beat it down to the neighborhood. Arrived just in time, too."

Jamal turned left at the next light. "Anyway, when he arrived, there was already a situation goin' down. A couple of guys were threatening Frankie with knives, and Father Joe stepped between them and Frankie. Father Joe tried to talk some sense into the guys, but one thing led to another, and Father Joe got sliced."

Jamal turned into a large parking area and eased the van into an empty space. Beth stared at the multilevel structure before her. A large sign across the face of the building read "Sisters of Bethlehem Charity Hospital."

As he turned off the engine, Jamal continued.

"Father Joe managed to disarm and hold the guy who sliced him, but the other one took off just before the police arrived."

Jamal stepped from the van and managed to open Beth's door by the time she had unbuckled her seat belt. "Come on," he said to Beth, "I'll take you to him."

They entered the emergency room amid total chaos. At least that is how it appeared at first, but then Beth realized it was at least an orderly chaos. Jamal walked beside her, his hand lightly at her back. He guided her past the reception desk and toward the examining rooms. Several people greeted him by name, and Jamal smiled and returned their greetings.

"You seem well known here," Beth remarked.

Jamal flashed his now familiar smile. "Been a patient here more times than I care to remember. Until Father Joe straightened me out. Now I bring the business."

Beth frowned.

"I'm an EMT. Work on one of the ambulances part-time. Helps me pay for medical school."

Beth stopped. "You're going to medical school?"

Pride shone in Jamal's eyes. "Yep. Thanks to Father Joe and a scholarship or two. Next year I hope to be an intern here."

"That's wonderful!"

"Yeah. Who'd have guessed."

Beth's face reddened. "I didn't mean anything by—"

"I did." Jamal grinned at her.

Urging her forward a few more steps, Jamal stopped in front of a curtained-off examination area. "Father Joe, you decent?"

"I'm decent," came Joe's familiar voice.

Jamal moved the curtain aside for Beth to enter and followed her into the small space. Joe slipped off the examination table when they entered. He was stripped to the waist, and a gauze bandage circled his midsection, a dark red spot tainting the bandage on his left side.

"Yo, Pops," Jamal greeted Joe. "Brought you a visitor."

"About time," returned Joe as he smiled at Beth. "Hi. Sorry I couldn't pick you up myself."

She stared at the crimson stain on the gauze bandage around Joe's midriff.

~20~

*B*eth fought back her tears and panic at the thought Joe had unquestioningly risked his life for one of his boys. She lost her battle when a couple of tears trickled down her cheeks.

"Whoa, no sense getting upset," Joe told her. "I'm fine. No great harm done. I'll be good as new in a few days."

Dried blood spotted his jeans, and in spite of his attempt at nonchalance, he looked pale.

"You're not fine," she admonished. "You've been wounded, and . . . and . . ." She swiped at the wetness on her face.

"I'll be waitin' outside," Jamal offered and closed the curtain behind him.

When Jamal was gone, Joe gathered Beth into his arms and held her. She let her tears flow for a few moments. When she calmed down, Joe held her at arms' length and wiped the dampness from her face. He handed her a tissue from a box nearby and let her blow her nose.

"I'm sorry," she said. "I shouldn't have broken down like that. It's just that . . ." She laid her hand against his face. "You look so pale. Are you sure you're all right?"

"I'm fine," he reassured her. "A little tender on one side, that's all."

"Oh, I'm sorry. When I hugged you, did it

hurt?"

"I didn't notice a thing."

"Don't lie, Joe. It doesn't suit you."

His eyes grew dark. "I noticed how good it felt to hold you in my arms." He gathered her against him again and rested his head against hers. "I've missed you, Beth. I've been worried about you and wondering how you've been."

"I've mis—"

"Well, now, let's get you re—" The large black woman in hospital greens stopped mid-step. "Sorry Joe, didn't know you had company."

He smiled and released Beth. "That's okay, Gracie. No harm done. I'd like you to meet Beth Stevens, a friend of mine from Colorado."

Gracie nodded and smiled at Beth. "Nice to meet you. Joe said he was expecting you. Didn't see you come in."

"I just got here." Beth felt like she had been caught with her hand in the cookie jar.

"Beth and I grew up next door to each other" Joe said. "She's like a little sister to me, Gracie."

"If you say so, Joe." Gracie winked at him and grinned. "Dr. Carson wants you to get this prescription filled, and he told me to make you promise to take all of it. If you don't, you'll have to answer to me and Jamal. Got that?"

"Got it."

"There's also one here for pain. Be sure and fill it, too, and use it as needed. Now if you'll drop your britches I'll give you your tetanus shot and you can be on your way."

Beth stifled a grin at the fear rising in Joe's eyes. "Can't you forget this one? I'm sure I'm up to date on my shots."

"Doctor's orders. No telling where that knife

has been. Now bend over."

"I think I'll find Jamal." Beth giggled and slipped between the curtains.

~21~

*J*amal stopped the van in the driveway of a large Victorian house in need of fresh paint. A well-manicured lawn and two huge eucalyptus trees gave way to an expansive covered porch. A tall board fence surrounded the backyard, obscuring Beth's view of what lay beyond. From the garage next to the house, she could hear pounding and the whine of an electric saw.

Music blared from the living room as Joe

opened the front door and ushered Beth inside. Several boys lounged on the sofa, chairs, and floor amid a jumble of books and papers. The clinking of dishes drifted from the kitchen.

As soon as Joe entered the living room, one of the boys jumped up and shut off the stereo. Quiet permeated the room as the boys stared at Joe and Beth.

"Yo, Pops, how ya doin'?" The greeting came from a boy sprawled in an easy chair.

"Where are your manners? We have a guest, in case you haven't noticed."

Half a dozen boys scrambled to their feet, looking sheepish, some rubbing their hands on their baggy trousers, others gathering up papers and books. Beth fought back a chuckle and smiled warmly as each boy was introduced. The six boys were as varied in age and ethnic background as their names indicated—Rashan, Alex, Javier, Tyrone, Lucas, and Miguel.

"You get patched up okay?" Miguel asked, worry showing in his eyes.

"Twenty-five stitches," Joe answered. "I guess wrestling with you guys is out for a while."

"No sweat, Pops. We've been beatin' up on ya, anyway," bragged Tyrone.

"You wish." Joe winked.

"Whoa, listen to that," Alex said. "Pops thinks he's large and in charge."

The other boys laughed, and Joe smiled. "Better practice up." he said. "As soon as the stitches are out, I'll be more than happy to prove it to you."

"Sure, Pops," echoed around the room.

"Where's Frankie?" Joe asked, putting a stop to the banter.

"Up in his room, chillin,'" Rashan said. "He's

been stewin' ever since he got home 'bout what happened. I think he's all like afraid you're gonna kick him out. Ya want me to go get 'im?"

Joe frowned. "No. Let him think about it a while longer. Anyway, I think Jamal's up there now. I'll deal with Frankie later. Right now, I'm going to show Mrs. Stevens around."

"Nice meetin' ya, Mrs. Stevens," Tyrone said.

"Call me Beth. Please." She smiled when she saw the hesitation in his eyes.

"Sure." He grinned at her. "Long as it's okay with Pops.

"It's okay."

In the kitchen, Beth met Omar, Ramon, and Josh. They were elbow deep in lunch dishes. Then Joe ushered her outside. He hesitated at the door to the garage.

"Each one of the boys has specific chores to

do, inside and out, and they all take turns. Since we lost our housekeeper, the boys help with the cleaning, fix most of the meals, and do the laundry. I supervise, except on Saturday night. Then it's my turn to cook."

Joe grinned at Beth and her heart skipped a beat. "Care to help me fix supper tonight?"

"Is that why you invited me here?" She tried to keep the smile off her face and out of her eyes.

"Absolutely," he said. "My cooking stinks." His grin spread further across his face.

"Okay, but it'll cost you."

"I was afraid of that. How much?"

"I'm not sure. I'll let you know."

"Just remember, I'm poor."

Joe opened the door to the garage. Two boys stood at a workbench, their backs to Beth and Joe. The boys turned at the thud of the door closing.

They both greeted Joe with the now familiar

"Yo, Pops." Joe introduced Juan and Moises to Beth, then explained what they were working on.

"We make cradles," Joe said.

~22~

*T*he warmth in Joe's voice spoke volumes about the importance of the cradles. "Every one of the boys works on the cradles when he has spare time," he said. "There's almost always somebody out here working. Moises, Juan, Rashan, and Lucas are all old enough to run the saws. The younger boys do the sanding, staining, and varnishing.

"When a cradle is complete, all of the boys can take pride in being a part of the finished product.

Finished cradles are taken to Bethlehem Charity
Hospital and given to needy families of new babies. A
few are taken to the shelters for battered women, and
some to the Teen Moms program the diocese runs.
We never seem to run out of a need for them."

Juan reached under the workbench and set a
finished cradle on the cement floor at Beth's feet. He
smoothed his fingers in gentle movements over the
wooden cradle and the carved heart with a cross in the
center as he explained each step required to make the
cradle.

"Pops designed the cradles, including the
heart and cross in the middle of each end. Sometimes
we add a little variation on our own, but the original
design is always there." Juan set the cradle rocking
when he finished.

Beth knelt and smoothed her hand along the
edge of the cradle. Tears filled her eyes. She thought

of the tiny life growing inside her, and imagined her baby in the cradle.

"It's the most beautiful cradle I've ever seen," she said. "The babies that get these are very lucky."

She rose and smiled at the two boys. "You should be proud of what you're doing here. What a precious gift you're giving."

They both smiled.

"Workin' on the cradles helps us express ourselves," Moises said, "and keeps us busy enough so we ain't—" Beth saw him glance at Joe, "aren't out on the streets doin' sh . . . stuff."

"My sister got one of the cradles," Juan said. "It was sweet knowin' I helped build it."

"Gifts made with love are always the best gifts," Beth said. "And I can see the love that's gone into this cradle." She thought she saw Juan blush a little.

"Three years ago," Joe said, "Juan's sister was fifteen, pregnant, and scared. Through the Teen Moms program, she's gotten a fresh start, finished high school, and is in a nursing program."

"Thanks to Father Joe. He helped her a lot. Just like he's helped me." The smile Juan directed at Joe reflected volumes of love and respect.

Joe clamped a hand on Juan's shoulder. "You did most of it by yourself, Juan. I just pointed you in the right direction." Joe gave Juan's shoulder a squeeze.

"So, Pops, you okay?"

"No major harm done. I'll live."

Beth flinched at Joe's casual comment. She knew the situation had been more serious than he let on.

"Good, 'cause we need you," Juan said.

Juan's candidness surprised Beth, until she

realized Joe had demonstrated the kind of love to these boys that made them comfortable and secure in their own feelings. She was beginning to understand the importance of Joe's calling.

Moises glanced at Joe's blood-spotted jeans and ripped and bloody shirt, and in his best gangster voice, asked, "You want we should work Frankie over for ya?" He grinned as he said it.

Joe smiled. "You know the drill. Group meeting after supper to discuss the punishment for breaking a rule."

Joe ushered Beth outside, but before they entered the house, Beth stopped.

"You're not going to let Frankie stew much longer, are you? It sounds like he's scared to death over what happened."

"He should be. He could have gotten killed."

"Do you think he really understands that? He

was thinking about his friend."

"He wasn't thinking at all. Yes, he understands. And no, I'm not going to let him stew much longer. If I do, he's liable to bolt on me. I'm sorry I have to deal with this while you're here. I should be spending the time with you."

"Frankie's more important. I'll see if I can help the other boys do something."

Joe smiled. "Javier is having trouble with his English. He was born in L.A., but his family is from Mexico. His mother speaks very little English. He's living with us because his father is in prison, and his mother wasn't able to cope. Javier got picked up on petty theft charges—part of gang orientation. He's a good boy. Just needs some love and direction." Joe winked. "And help with his English."

"I'll see what I can do," Beth said.

~23~

*J*oe met Jamal on the stairs. "He's packed and ready to go," warned Jamal. "I don't think I did much to convince him to stay."

"Thanks, Jamal, for everything you did today."

"Anytime, Pops. 'Course you should know that by now."

"I suppose I do." Joe smiled. Jamal was the first boy he'd rescued. The confident young man who stood next to him on the stairs barely resembled the angry teenager he'd known years ago.

"You're welcome to stay for supper," Joe said.

"Trying to get out of cooking again, aren't you?"

Joe chuckled. "I think I've got Beth talked into that chore. How about it? The boys always enjoy having you here."

"Can't. My shift starts in thirty minutes."

They parted, Joe going up the stairs, Jamal down. Jamal stopped at the bottom of the stairs.

"Hey Pops." Joe turned toward Jamal. "Beth's all right. Or as my brothers would say, 'she's fine as wine.'" He grinned at Joe.

Joe smiled. "Yes, she is."

Joe stood in the doorway, watching the hunched figure sitting on the edge of the bed with his back to Joe. Frankie was the newest addition to the family. Like most of the boys at the Asylum, by the time he was twelve, Frankie had seen the worst side of life—more than most people saw in a lifetime. Frankie had lived at the Asylum for five months. Two weeks earlier they had celebrated his thirteenth birthday.

Frankie sniffed and wiped his sleeve across his nose. Joe sat on the bed across from Frankie and handed him a Kleenex.

"Rough day," Joe said.

Frankie glanced at Joe and took in his still bloody clothes. He blew his nose and stared at the floor.

"Jamal says you're all packed and ready to go."

"I think I got everything," Frankie mumbled, his eyes trained on the carpet between them.

"So where are you going?"

Frankie shrugged his shoulders. "I don't know."

"Frankie, look at me."

Frankie slowly lifted his head.

"This is your home. Why would you want to go somewhere else?"

"'Cause I don't deserve to stay here. I screwed up." He sucked in a breath. "And I almost got you killed."

Joe's heart broke as Frankie fought back sobs.

"You almost got yourself killed, Frankie. How would that have helped your friend?"

Frankie returned his attention to the floor. "I don't know," he mumbled.

"What happened? What caused you to break the first rule of this house?"

"Tony called me. He was all like scared and

pumped. Said he had a gun and was gonna get initiated tonight. I tried to talk him outa doin' it, but he wouldn't listen. I thought if I talked to him, face to face, he'd listen."

"Why didn't you call me? I always have my cell phone."

"I tried, but you didn't answer, and I couldn't wait. When I called the shelter, they said you'd left. I told Miguel where I was going. He said I should wait for you."

"He was right. The first rule, Frankie, is when something goes down you wait to talk to me. You don't try to handle it yourself."

"I know." New tears streaked down his face. He slipped off the bed and picked up a duffel bag next to his feet. "See ya around Pops. Thanks for everything."

Joe leaned forward and rested his arms on his

legs. Frankie was halfway to the door before Joe spoke.

"Still determined to leave?"

Frankie stopped, but did not turn around. "Saves you and the guys having to kick me out."

Joe rose and blocked Frankie's path to the door. He relieved Frankie of the duffel and set it aside. Placing his hands on Frankie's shoulders, Joe waited until Frankie looked at him.

"We're a family, Frankie. Just because somebody screws up, doesn't mean we kick him out of the family. That's not the way it works. There are consequences to what you did, but sending you away isn't one of them. Understand?"

"Y-you mean I can stay?" The hope in Frankie's eyes tore at Joe's heart.

"I mean you're expected to stay." Joe watched as Frankie fought back his sobs. Joe gathered Frankie into his arms. "If you want to cry, it's all right. Crying doesn't make you weak, Frankie. There are times when it's acceptable. This is one of those times."

Frankie's shoulders shuddered against Joe's chest as the young boy gave in to his sobs.

~24~

After helping Frankie unpack, Joe washed up and dressed in a clean shirt and jeans. He found Beth at the kitchen table with Javier, the two of them so intent on the English lesson, they didn't notice Joe watching them from the doorway. He leaned against the doorframe, closed his eyes, and listened to Beth's soothing voice explain proper sentence structure.

Joe grimaced as a sharp pain stabbed at his side. The localized anesthetic he was given at the hospital had worn off, and the wound throbbed. He took a deep breath and waited for the pain to subside, then smiled as he watched the light of understanding glow in Javier's eyes.

"I theenk I understand." Javier beamed at Beth. "You make it seem very easy. Thank you, Señora." He grinned at Beth.

"You're welcome, Javier."

"Got him all straightened out?" Joe asked as he approached the table.

"On the right track, anyway," Beth answered.

"Javier, take a break from lessons for a while."

"Sure thing, Pops." Javier gathered up his books. As he passed Joe, he raised his thumb and grinned. "Muy bonita, Pops. Belleza."

Joe smiled and sat in the chair Javier had vacated. "He thinks you are beautiful." He watched the blush spread across Beth's face. "He's right."

"He's a charmer," Beth commented. "How lucky you are to have all these boys." She smiled at Joe. "I understand more than ever why this is so important to you."

"I thought you might if you could meet them and see what we're doing here."

"How's Frankie?"

"He's going to be fine. He's discovered what being a part of a family is about." Beads of sweat broke out on Joe's forehead as another sharp pain pierced his side. "Do you know what Jamal did with those pain pills the doctor prescribed for me? The shot seems to be wearing off."

Beth rose and went to one of the cupboards. "He gave them to me, and I put them in here," she said as she retrieved a plastic vial from the shelf. "The antibiotics are here, too, when you need them."

She handed the pain pills to Joe along with a glass of water. "Maybe you should lie down for a while. I'll see to supper."

Joe swallowed a pill and stuffed the bottle in his jeans' pocket. "I'll be fine. And you're not obligated to cook supper."

"You're right. I'm not," she agreed, "but I'd like to. Do you think they could stomach my famous spaghetti?"

"I think if they know what's good for them, they'll eat it without complaint. Want some help?"

"If you're feeling up to it."

"Just tell me what to do. It'll keep my mind off the pain."

Beth had never enjoyed a meal so much. Table talk was lively, though sometimes argumentative. Whenever an argument appeared to get out of hand, Joe would intercede, and before long the combatants either reached an agreement or compromised. But even as they argued, Beth could see they respected each other.

Javier insisted on sitting by Beth, and each time Beth glanced his way, he would smile and wink. At the young age of eleven he already knew how to charm the ladies.

Frankie ate in silence, not joining in the talk unless asked a direct question. Although no one mentioned the knifing incident, Beth knew he was worried about the upcoming group meeting. According to Joe, the group decided on his punishment. Beth wanted to hold Frankie and assure him everything would be all right. He looked so young and vulnerable.

Beth marveled at the boys' voracious appetites. She thought she fixed far more spaghetti than the boys would eat, but Joe insisted they'd eat every morsel. As Joe predicted, when the meal was done, there were no leftovers.

All the boys helped with the cleanup, their banter making the work less burdensome. Once the last clean dish was put away, Joe suggested they adjourn to the living room for the group meeting. Joe invited Beth to be a part of the meeting, but she declined.

"I'll find some way to amuse myself," she said.

As the group left the kitchen, Moises clamped his hand on Frankie's shoulder and conjured up his gangster voice. "I say we hang him by da tumbs and let him rot."

Beth hoped Frankie noticed the humor in Moises' eyes when he said it.

~25~

*B*eth wandered outside and into the backyard. The area was much larger than she expected. Rose bushes bordered an expansive lawn, which gave way to a vegetable garden. Rows of carrots, peas, radishes, and a variety of plants as yet unrecognizable peeked through the soil.

Beth wandered among the roses, delighted at the varied shades of red, pink, orange, and white, and breathed in their sweet fragrance. Baby's breath grew in the spaces between the roses, giving the garden the effect of a large bouquet.

She thought again about Joe's remark that he was poor. As she fingered a coral-colored rose, Beth smiled. He was far from poor; he was rich. Joe's wealth was measured, not by monetary values, but by the love he gave and received.

Tears stung her eyes as she thought about the baby she carried. Once she told Joe she was pregnant, everything would change. Joe would do nothing less than what was right for her and the baby, but it would cost him what he had now. She was not ready to take all this away from him. Not yet. Maybe not ever.

She looked up at the darkening sky. "There must be a way, Father, for Joe to continue his work here and still be a father to his child and a husband to me. Gabe said with You all things are possible. Please find a way to make it all possible. Joe and the boys deserve nothing less."

She sat on a redwood bench that circled a large oak and leaned against the trunk, drawing her knees up against her. "I trust You, Father, to give us the answer. Let this precious gift be the building stone of something very special for all of us."

She thought about the cradles and the way Juan reacted when she told him that gifts made with love were always the best gifts. The child she carried in her womb was such a gift.

Beth hummed the tune of *The Best Gift*, a song she hadn't thought of in several years. She closed her eyes, and as she hummed, a feeling of peace enveloped her. She found herself singing the words halfway through the song. Like the words of the song, she knew the best gift was a tiny, newborn

"That's beautiful," Joe remarked. "I like hearing you sing."

Beth started at the sound of his voice and dropped her feet to the ground, resting her hands in her lap. He handed her a yellow rose and sat beside her. As Beth took the rose, Joe noticed a tear lingering on her cheek. He brushed it away and put his arm around her shoulders.

"I'm sorry Beth. I didn't realize seeing the cradles this afternoon would remind you of what can't be. I didn't mean to upset you."

She leaned her head on his shoulder. "You haven't upset me, Joe. On the contrary, being here has shown me what kind of man you are and the miracles you've accomplished. Making those cradles shows the boys the importance of doing unselfishly for others. How lucky they are to have you."

He kissed the top of her head. "You give me too much credit, Beth. What I've done here is because God has shown me what to do. This is His work, not mine."

"You've done a wonderful job of carrying out His work."

"Thanks."

"Did they decide on Frankie's punishment?"

"He's grounded for one month. I think it would have been stiffer, but for the fact he'll miss out on a basketball camp he had his heart set on. He'll miss seeing Shaquille O'Neal and Michael Jordan, among others. He'd been running errands for a local drugstore after school to help pay for it."

"Couldn't they ground him and still let him go

to the camp?"

"Moises pleaded Frankie's case for him. Quite well, I might add. But in the end, the boys felt the results of Frankie's actions warranted a strong message from them. There are consequences to breaking the rules. He's accepted his punishment. He's disappointed, but I've reassured him there's always next year. It's an annual event."

"Poor Frankie."

"He's learned a valuable lesson and will think twice before he breaks another rule. Don't feel too sorry for him. He's discovered how much he means to everyone."

They sat in silence for a while, her head on Joe's shoulder, his arm around her, and listened to the night sounds of the city and the music and laughter filtering from the house.

"I wish every night could be like this," Joe said. "You've brought softness into the house, and made it seem more like a home than it ever has before. The one thing the boys lack at the Asylum is the one thing I can't provide—a mother."

"You're doing a wonderful thing," Beth said. "You've given them a family and a father to look up to."

Joe gave her shoulder a squeeze. "I do love you, Beth," he whispered.

"I love you, too."

"I wish things could be different. I wish I hadn't hurt you."

"You haven't hurt me, Joe. You've given me the gift of love, and you've shown me the wonders love can accomplish."

~26~

*S*weat ran down Joe's face as he pulled weeds from around the radishes. Working in the garden or the workshop always helped Joe think things through when he was troubled, and he'd been troubled since Beth left Los Angeles two weeks earlier.

She seemed different. He couldn't put his finger on it, but she *was* different. Even though he'd spent only a few hours with her, he felt she was keeping something to herself, and that worried him.

Adding to his troubled thoughts was the naturalness of her presence in the household.

The boys accepted her without question. Joe explained, quite convincingly, he thought, that Beth was like a sister to him, but several of the boys teased him about making her a permanent resident of the Asylum.

"Why don't you marry her, Pops?" Rashan asked. "She'd fit right in. Be nice to have a lady around the house."

Joe accepted the teasing in good humor. Nevertheless, Rashan touched on a question Joe had asked himself over and over. Why did the Church frown on something so special between a man and a woman? Why would they not allow their priests to marry? Times were much different from when the law first went into effect centuries ago.

She belongs here. Yet I can't ask her to be a

part of this. Tell me, Father, what's so wrong about that?

Joe wiped the sweat from his face and stepped out of the garden. The sound of whistling turned his attention to the roses at the other end of the lawn. An older man stood among the blooms, working away with pruning shears, oblivious to Joe.

Joe approached the man. He hadn't seen or heard him enter the backyard.

"Excuse me, may I ask what you're doing here?" Joe questioned.

The whistling stopped and the man smiled at Joe. He removed a glove and offered his hand.

"Name's Gabe," he said. "I've been sent to help get this place in shape. The better it looks, the better price the diocese will get for it."

Joe stared. "I think you must be mistaken. This place is not for sale."

"This is Father Joe's Asylum, isn't it?"

"Yes, but—"

"Then this is the right place." Gabe removed his cap and smoothed down his thinning gray hair. He replaced the cap and focused his clear blue eyes on Joe's troubled face. "You must be Father Joe."

"I am, but that still doesn't explain what's going on here."

"It was my understanding you'd been told. From the look on your face, apparently not."

"I suggest you start explaining yourself before I call the police," Joe said.

"Well, I hate to be the bearer of bad news," Gabe said, "but according to my information, this house is being sold, and you're being reassigned. A church somewhere in the diocese." He shook his head. "Can't remember which one for sure."

"Reassigned? What do you mean reassigned?

What about the boys?" Joe struggled to keep his temper in check and the panic at bay. Gabe's nonchalant attitude fueled Joe's irritation.

"I believe they're to be farmed out to foster homes as soon as possible."

"Foster homes?" Fear and panic hit Joe full force. "They'll never survive in foster homes. I can't leave these kids to foster homes."

"I can't agree with you more, Joe, but unfortunately, the diocese doesn't see it our way."

Joe's knees weakened, and he sank onto the lawn, a knot forming in his stomach. "I'm being punished for my sin," he whispered.

"Punished? By whom?" Gabe asked.

"God," Joe croaked.

"Can't say as I agree with you there," Gabe said as he sat down beside Joe. "God isn't in the punishment business where His chosen are concerned. Not His style."

"Then why? Why would He do this?"

"Maybe He's trying to tell you something."

Joe glanced at Gabe. "And what would that be?"

"That there's more than one way to accomplish what God has planned for you." Gabe set the pruning shears on the ground and removed his other glove. "If you want to continue working with these kids, why don't you seek funding outside the Church? Don't be afraid to ask. There are plenty of rich people in the Los Angeles area needing a place to invest their money and provide them a tax deduction at the same time. Might as well be for your cause."

"But if the Church reassigns me . . ." Joe stared at the ground.

"The Church can't reassign you if you are no longer their priest."

"But my vows. Fifteen years ago I committed myself to God and His work."

"Your commitment is to God, not man." Gabe patted Joe's shoulder. "The final decision is yours, but don't wait too long." Gabe rose and stepped toward the roses. "By the way, Beth is pregnant."

Joe's head shot up. "*What?* How do you know—?"

Gabe was nowhere in sight. Joe rubbed his eyes, wondering if he had dreamed the whole conversation, or if he was suffering from sunstroke. But the gloves and pruning shears still lay on the grass where Gabe had set them.

~27~

Joe fought his temper and prayed for calm as he drove to diocese headquarters. By the time he was ushered into Bishop McKenzie's office, the full force of his anger exploded in the bishop's face.

Before Bishop McKenzie could utter a greeting, Joe planted his hands on the priest's desk and leaned toward him. "Why didn't you tell me you were considering selling the house and farming the boys out to foster homes? I should have been consulted before *any* decision was made!"

"*Sit down*, Father Connor."

Joe's jaw tightened, his hands still planted on the desk. "Answer my question."

Bishop McKenzie pushed his chair away from the desk and stood. "Either sit down so we can discuss this rationally, or leave until you've calmed down. The choice is yours."

Joe closed his eyes and took a deep breath. He realized he was doing exactly what he tried to teach his boys not to do. He reacted out of anger, instead of thinking things through and then taking action when he was calmer. He pushed away from the desk and sank onto a chair behind him.

Bishop McKenzie sat and nodded at Joe. "That's better, Father. Now, how did you know about the house and the boys?"

Joe took another deep breath and clenched his

fists. He was still shaking, inside and out. "The gardener you sent over told me. He was under the impression I already knew."

Bishop McKenzie frowned. "I didn't send any gardener over."

"Gabe said he'd been sent to help get the house ready." A strange sensation swept over Joe. He shook his head. "It doesn't matter how I found out," Joe said. "I'd say from your reaction it's true."

"I planned to stop by the house tonight to talk to you and the boys. I'm sorry you found out from someone else."

"Why?" Joe frowned. "Why are you doing this?"

"The diocese is facing a financial downturn right now. Contributions are down. Programs must be cut. We've tried to keep as many as we can, but we can no longer finance all of them. The cost of the new cathedral is more than we anticipated, and many of the contributions we've received are designated for it. The decision to cut your program wasn't an easy one. I'm sorry."

"Can't you see the good that's come out of this program? Look how many boys have been given a real chance at life because the Church made a place for them. You can't cut them off now."

Joe leaned forward in his chair. "The very first boy I took in is in medical school. Look how much good he'll be able to do as a doctor. Another boy is a policeman, and two more are teaching. They're in professions where they can reach kids and change lives. It's already happened many times over."

"I've never questioned the success of your program. But you reach only a few boys at a time. Our homeless shelters help dozens of people at a time. And those shelters are demanding more and more of our resources. I've looked for ways to save what you're doing, but I've found none."

"Besides you, who was involved in the decision?"

"No one. The responsibility is mine and mine alone. And I did not make the decision lightly. A great deal of thought and prayer went into it. After the knifing incident two weeks ago, I felt the time had come to move you on to other things. I can't afford to lose experienced priests."

"I wasn't hurt that bad." Joe rubbed his hand over his face. "I was never in any real danger. I've taken self-defense classes and keep up to date with my training."

"Father Connor, no one is invincible. What if the weapon had been a gun? I think it's time for things to change."

"The boys, even some of the gangs, have

learned to trust me. They know me." Panic surfaced, and Joe saw the last ten years of hard work slipping away.

"Even if you don't want me overseeing the program anymore, foster homes are not the answer. I could train a younger priest to take my place." Unable to sit still any longer, Joe stood and paced, his mind racing, searching for some way to make Bishop McKenzie change his mind. "With the Church's backing, I'm sure I can find grant money somewhere to pick up the slack. I'll just need a little time to do it." Joe hated begging, but he was desperate. "Bishop McKenzie, please, just a little more time."

"Father Connor, let it go. The truth is that in light of the recent scandals concerning some priests and their alleged misuse of young boys, it doesn't look good for a priest to be living in a house full of young men. We can't afford any more allegations."

Joe's face reddened. "I have *never* molested any boys. I would *never* do that. You can't cut my program because of the actions of a few sick men. I'm helping these boys, not hurting them. *Please reconsider.*"

"The decision has been made. The house won't be sold until all the boys have been placed somewhere. That will give you time to help the boys adjust to the change. When the last boy is gone, you'll be assigned a parish church." Bishop McKenzie leaned forward and picked up a folder from his desk. "Now if you'll excuse me, I have a great deal of work to do."

Joe's anger surfaced again, and he fought the urge to throttle the man sitting behind the massive desk. After a moment, Joe stormed from the office, slamming the door behind him.

~28~

*H*is knuckles white from clutching the steering wheel, Joe drove aimlessly through Los Angeles. To add to his frustration and worry, Gabe's final words played over and over in his mind. "Beth is pregnant."

An hour later, Joe found himself at the Plaza in downtown Los Angeles, home of Our Lady Queen of Angels Church. Needing a quiet place to think and pray, he parked the van and walked the short distance to the oldest church in the city.

Prayer was a powerful weapon, and in his disappointment and rage over Bishop McKenzie's decision, Joe nearly abandoned his most effective tool. God never failed to answer a prayer, but sometimes God's answers came slowly, or in an unexpected way. Joe had prayed for weeks without an answer to his dilemma over Beth, and now he faced an additional problem. He didn't have the luxury of time to save the haven he labored so long to establish for troubled boys.

As Joe entered the empty church, the whispered prayers of generations swirled around him and tugged at the bitterness Joe harbored in his heart. Clenching his hands together and fighting against his still seething anger, Joe knelt to pray.

"Father, how can Bishop McKenzie so arbitrarily dismiss these kids and their needs? He said he prayed about it, but did he really listen to Your counsel, or was his mind already made up?

"My life's work is disintegrating before my eyes. And if that's not enough, according to this Gabe character, Beth's pregnant. Impossible. Or is Gabe right about that, too? Is that what was bothering Beth when she was here two weeks ago? Why she reacted to the cradles the way she did?"

Joe scrubbed his hands over his face and took a deep breath. "What's happening Father? Is Beth afraid to tell me, or has she chosen not to for other reasons? Father," he cried, "I'm confused and lost, and I don't know where to go or what to do anymore." A tear slid down his cheek. "Please, help me." He sucked in a deep breath and exhaled.

"How much more will you punish me? I've asked for Your forgiveness, Father. I've dedicated my life to Your church and Your work, but that's being snatched away from me.

"Why are you pulling me away from everything I've trained for? Why did you bring Beth and me together again, after all these years, when you know I can't marry her?"

Joe squelched angry words rising in his throat and took another deep breath. "If I walk away from the priesthood, what does that say to the boys about commitment? If I don't marry Beth, what kind of mixed message am I giving the boys? If you must punish me, Father, then I accept that. But don't punish my boys. Or Beth. They've done *nothing* to deserve this."

Joe lifted his face toward the ornate ceiling. "If there's some way to salvage this, then show me, Father. Tell me how. I need to hear Your voice."

Light filtered from the windows and illuminated dust motes suspended in the air. "*Now,*

181

Father. I need answers *now*." He clenched his fists
and demanded, "*Answer me.*" Guilt for shouting at
God washed over Joe, and he softened his voice.
"*Please.*"

His head dropped, and he bit back an angry
oath.

Be still and know that I am God.

"Psalm 46," Joe whispered. "God is our
refuge and strength, an ever present help in trouble."
He closed his eyes and waited.

"Knew I'd find you here."

Startled, Joe turned toward the voice, unaware
of Gabe's presence until he spoke. Gabe placed his
hand on Joe's shoulder and knelt beside him.

"I take it what I told you is true?"

"You mean about the house and the boys?"
Gabe's appearance the moment Joe had pleaded for an
answer surprised him. He wondered how Gabe knew

he was here.

"For starters," Gabe replied.

"Yes, it's true. Just as you said."

"You know, my poor old knees can't take this kneeling for too long. Why don't we sit for a minute?"

Joe crossed himself and joined Gabe on a nearby bench.

Gabe smiled. "So you want an answer, do you? Look within, Joe. Your answer must first come from within, son. Listen."

The comment was not the answer Joe expected, but something made him want to listen to Gabe's counseling. Joe hardly knew this man, yet he trusted Gabe without knowing why.

"I'm listening," Joe said and leaned forward, resting his arms on his legs.

"You want to continue to work with the boys," Gabe commented, "but if you remain with the

183

Church, that will be taken away. And if you remain a priest, you can't marry Beth and be a father to your child.

"Just because God closed a door, doesn't mean He's punishing you. You need to look for the new door that He's opened and beckoning you through. Perhaps it's time you stepped away from the priesthood."

Joe looked at Gabe. "Is that what God wants me to do?"

Gabe smiled and placed his hand on Joe's shoulder. "You have responsibilities, Joe. All your children need you."

Joe shook his head. "How do I do it all? I've relied on the Church for so long."

"Then it's time you relied on God." Gabe reached in his shirt pocket and pulled out a small folded paper. He handed it to Joe. "This is a list of people who will help you. Start with the first one on the list. He'll be expecting you. Don't sell yourself short, Joe. You're a talented carpenter, and you can put those skills to good use.

"Trust God, Joe. He will guide you." Gabe rose and walked a few steps away. "Oh, one more thing. The child Beth carries is the child Father Rameriz spoke of in his prophecy. This is your destiny, Joe. Remember, all things are possible with God, and miracles do happen."

Joe lingered in the church long after Gabe departed, meditating on everything Gabe said. And as he did, the peace of God surrounded him and comforted him. When he arrived at the Asylum, he knew his course of action. All he required was for the boys to understand and accept his decision and the changes that would come with it.

When supper was over, Joe called a group

meeting. Before joining the boys, Joe prayed for courage and the right words to explain what had transpired over the last few months and the effect it would have on all of them. Then he took a deep breath and stepped into the living room. An expectant silence greeted him.

"This isn't easy for me," Joe began.

~29~

*J*oe sat in the van and stared at the expansive
mansion's ornate door. He was unaccustomed to
begging. On the long drive to this exclusive section of
Los Angeles he practiced what he was going to say.
But as he stared at the imposing mansion before him,
his mind went blank.

"Father, give me the words and the strength to
do this. It's for the boys, not me," he prayed.

As his hand reached for his briefcase, the door

to the house opened. A man in his mid-forties stepped out and walked toward Joe.

"Father Joe?" he asked, offering his hand as Joe stepped from the van. "I'm Paul Silverstein."

"Y-yes," Joe stuttered and shook the man's hand. His grip was strong and warm.

"Come in, please. I'm glad to finally get the chance to meet you. My gardener, Gabe, told me a lot about you, and I've looked forward to our meeting."

"Your gardener?"

"Yes. I thought you knew him."

"Y-yes, of course. I just didn't realize he was your gardener."

"Best I've ever had. My gardens have flourished under his care. I haven't been able to talk him out of leaving, though. Says he needs to move on, before his restless spirit stagnates." Paul chuckled. "I'm a bit envious of his freedom to come and go as he pleases."

He ushered Joe through the house to an expansive study. Joe settled into a soft leather chair opposite an oak desk and studied his host.

Although he stood only five foot nine, Paul Silverstein had an imposing presence. His graying hair fell in unruly curls across his forehead, which he repeatedly smoothed back several times before he and Joe reached the study. Paul nodded as he sat in the high-backed chair behind the desk, adjusted his eyeglasses, and leaned back.

"Gabe couldn't say enough about you and your Asylum, I believe he called it. Would you like to tell me about it?" When Joe failed to respond right away, Paul continued. "That's why you're here, isn't it? To find a way to support the house and the boys that live there?"

"Y-yes." Joe realized he must sound like an

idiot. All he had done since arriving was stutter over one word. He cleared his throat and hoped he could at least form an intelligent sentence or two before he was ushered out the door.

"I think the first thing I should do is clarify something," he began. "Father Joe is inappropriate, since I'm no longer a priest in the Catholic Church. Just call me Joe."

"All right."

"And secondly, I'm not here asking for anything for myself. I'm a pretty good carpenter and should be able to support myself doing odd jobs, building and repairing things for people. However, I doubt that will be enough to support twelve boys and their needs, or buy the house we're currently living in. I wouldn't ask, except these boys deserve a chance to make something of their lives. We've already successfully changed the lives of several boys."

Joe shifted in his chair. "The first boy I took in is now in medical school, and others have become teachers and policemen."

"Fa . . . Joe," Paul said. "When Gabe first told me about you, I did some checking. I'm extremely impressed with what you've done, not only with these boys, but also your work with the gangs. You're to be commended."

"What I've done is show them God's love. And though I'm no longer a priest, I will continue to teach them about God's love. And show them a way to a better life."

"That's plenty." Paul rose and moved to the front of his desk, settling on its edge. "I've been making movies for almost twenty years. I began by directing, then moved into producing my own movies. Quite frankly, I've made millions by investing in ideas I knew would produce results. And

I knew those ideas would produce results because I did my research.

"What I've discovered in researching you and your program is you get results, and those results are paying off. Not monetarily, but more importantly, in making our city a better place, one boy at a time."

Paul cleared his throat. "I've got more money than I know what to do with. My wife and kids are set for life. They'll never have to worry about their future. But you help boys who can't see what tomorrow will bring, let alone what their future holds. You don't have to sell me on your needs. We just have to figure out how much it will take, and how we're going to set things up, so the boys you're helping today, and the ones you'll help tomorrow, will know they have a secure future."

Paul stood and nodded toward the briefcase Joe had set beside his chair. "Now, why don't you show me what it will take to buy the house and support these boys, and then we can decide how many people we want in on this and what it will take to make it work."

Joe grabbed the briefcase, and as he set it on the desk, he offered a silent prayer of thanks.

~30~

With a cup of chamomile tea, Beth settled in the overstuffed chair nearest the picture window and watched the sun sink behind the Colorado National Monument. Rain clouds loomed along the horizon reflecting the brilliant golds, oranges, bright pinks, and maroons of the setting sun and promising another thunderstorm before the night ended.

The day had been unusually cool for mid-June, but Beth didn't mind. She loved thunderstorms, and the day had produced several, leaving behind the fresh scent of washed earth.

"Lord, how am I going to tell Joe about the baby?" she whispered. "What will he do when he finds out?" But she knew the answer. Joe would do the only thing he could. He would insist on marrying her. "And when he does, will he resent the fact that this baby caused him to give up his life's work?"

Moisture gathered in her eyes, and then she smiled. Joe was not the kind of man who held grudges. Once he made a decision, he never looked back. She had always known that about him. He hadn't changed and wouldn't now. But was the cost too high? She wanted him in her life, but she didn't want to take him away from his boys.

Knowing she could no longer put off the inevitable, she walked to the desk and picked up the phone. Saying another prayer for courage, she dialed

Joe's number.

"Father Joe's Asylum. Jamal speaking."

"Jamal? This is Beth. Is Joe there?"

"Beth. What a surprise." Jamal hesitated, and Beth felt uneasy. "Uh, Joe's not here. He's out of town. Is something wrong?"

"Nothing's wrong. I just needed to talk to him. Do you know when he'll be back?"

"I'm not sure. It could be anywhere from a few days to a couple of weeks."

"Oh." Hoping to hide the disappointment in her voice, Beth forced a smile to her face and laughed. "Well, wouldn't you know he'd be gone when I wanted to say 'hi.' Will you tell him I called when he gets back?"

"Sure thing. Do you want him to call you?"

Beth took a deep breath and let it out. "Sure, if he wants to. That would be fine."

"Will do. So, how've you been?" Jamal asked.

"Fine." Beth asked him about medical school, and they visited a few minutes longer before Beth replaced the phone. She sagged against the desk and gave in to the tears she forced back while talking to Jamal.

"Oh, Joe, I finally work up the nerve to call you, and you're out of town." Anger welled up along with the tears. "How *could* you? Now I've got to work up to this all over again. It's not *fair*."

The doorbell interrupted her tirade. "Great. That's all I need right now. Maybe I can pretend I'm not home." But she knew that was impossible. The living room curtains were still open, and several lights burned throughout the house.

Beth wiped the wetness from her cheeks with her palms and grabbed a tissue, blowing her nose as she moved to answer the insistent ringing. She yanked the door open, prepared to tell the unhappy caller she was not interested, and found herself face to face with Joe. Shock at seeing him left her speechless.

"Hi," he said and grinned.

The realization he stood on her porch dawned slowly. "Joe? I just tried to call you. Jamal said you were out of town."

"That depends on what you mean by 'out of town.' I'm definitely not in Los Angeles, so if that's what you're talk—" He frowned. "Beth, are you all right?"

She took a deep breath. "I-I don't know. I'm surprised." She ran a hand through her hair.

"May I come in?" he asked.

"Of course." She unlocked the screen door and held it open. "I'm sorry. I just didn't expect . . . What are you doing here?"

He set a suitcase inside the door and gathered

her into his arms. "First things first," he said and kissed her.

~31~

*T*he moment he took Beth in his arms, peace settled over Joe. Warmth surged through him as he savored the taste of her lips. Her arms slipped around his neck, and she melted against him, returning his kiss with equal passion.

When their lips parted, he smiled down at her and at the question he saw in her eyes. Pressing her head against his shoulder, he kissed her cheek and whispered in her ear, "I love you, Beth. Marry me."

He felt her go still in his arms and held his breath. Beth pushed away from him and looked into his eyes.

"What did you say?"

"I said, I love you, Beth. Marry me."

"That's what I thought you said." New tears welled in her eyes. "Are you serious?"

Joe cradled her face in his hands. "I've never been more serious in my life. I've walked away from the priesthood, Beth, with God's blessing. I'm free to marry you."

"Oh, Joe. You've dedicated your life to the Church, to your work, and to God. Are you sure?"

"I walked away from my vows to the Church, not God, and not my work. Yes, I'm sure." He stroked her cheeks with his thumbs. "So, what's your answer?"

Beth closed her eyes. "There's something you

need to know."

"That you're pregnant? I already know about the baby." He smiled and kissed the tip of her nose. "Some miracle, huh?"

Beth stared wide-eyed at him. As her knees gave way, Joe caught her around the waist and lifted her into his arms. He set her on the couch, sat beside her, and pulled her against him.

"You okay now?"

Beth took a deep breath. "I-I think so." She sat forward and turned to look at him. "How did you know? I haven't told anyone. Only my doctor and I know. Did he call you?"

"No." Joe grinned and pulled her against him again. "Let me tell you about a man named Gabe."

Beth gasped and looked up at Joe. "You know Gabe?"

Joe frowned at her. "Wiry, short guy, thin

graying hair, blue eyes that look into your soul?"

"That's him! But how—?"

"I should have known." Joe chuckled and shook his head. "The guy sure gets around."

Joe related everything that happened since Beth visited him in Los Angeles. She listened patiently, asking few questions.

"Paul and eleven of his friends bought the house and set up a trust fund that will oversee the running of the Asylum. The twelve investors make up the board that will oversee what I'm doing. In spite of that, I've been given complete control over the trust. There's enough money in the trust that the interest will fund our needs, and we'll never have to touch the principle. We may eventually expand to include more boys. And someday maybe girls. Right now, we're taking it one day at a time."

Joe kissed Beth's forehead. "God works in

mysterious ways, his wonders to perform," he said, almost in a whisper.

After a moment or two of silence, Beth asked, "Do your investors know about me?"

"They know everything. I've been completely up front with them. They're anxious to meet you."

"I hope I don't disappoint them."

"Believe me, Beth, you won't." He kissed her, then asked, "So, how about it? You willing to take a chance on an ex-priest and his crazy dreams, not to mention a house full of boys?"

"Whither thou goest," she answered. "Yes. I'll take you on, the boys, and anything you choose to get me involved in."

Her laugh was smothered in another kiss as they sealed a lifetime promise of love and adventure.

~32~

*T*he next few days were a flurry of activity.
Beth listed her home with a real estate agent, insisting
that when the house sold, the money from the sale
and the estate her first husband left her would be put
in trust for the baby she carried. Decisions also had to
be made on what household items would go to Los
Angeles with them, and which items they would give
to charity. Beth set a few things aside to give to
friends.

When Beth broke the news of her impending marriage to her doctor and friend, Alan, he was understandably skeptical. But Joe's frankness and obvious love for Beth put Alan's fears to rest. Alan's only regret was that he would not see Beth's pregnancy through to the birth. To his surprise, Beth insisted that even though she would be seeing a doctor in Los Angeles, she wanted Alan present at the birth. He promised he would do his best.

On Wednesday morning, Beth and Joe applied for a marriage license, and on Thursday morning, they met with Beth's minister, the Reverend John Thomas.

"It was a surprise when Beth called and asked me if I would marry you," Reverend Thomas commented as the three of them settled in the church office. Reverend Thomas addressed his next remark to Joe. "I had no idea Beth was even involved with anyone, so you can imagine my surprise when she told me her fiancé is a former priest."

Turning to Beth, he continued. "If you don't mind, Beth, I'd like to talk to Joe alone for a while. It's a serious issue when a man leaves the priesthood. I'd like to address the issue with Joe before I talk to you together. Perhaps you could do some shopping for an hour or so, then come back." He smiled at Beth. "I hope you understand."

"If she doesn't, I do," Joe said. "I would have been disappointed had you reacted otherwise, Reverend Thomas."

Beth smiled and rose. "In that case, I'll take this opportunity to let my boss at the library know the leave of absence I have taken will be permanent."

When Beth left, Joe spoke. "Well, Reverend Thomas, I'm sure you'd like to know if my leaving the priesthood is going to come back to haunt me. And if, in the future, I'll not only regret my decision, but blame Beth because I can no longer administer the rituals of my church."

Reverend Thomas nodded. "I hadn't planned on putting it quite so bluntly, but yes, that's exactly what I want to know. However, it's far more complicated than what you've summed up in a sentence or two." He leaned back in his chair. "And call me John. Reverend Thomas is much too formal."

Joe smiled and relaxed. "All right, John. To set your mind at ease, I'll tell you a little about my background, my history with Beth, and my service in the Church. And then I'm going to tell you about the unusual events that have transpired over the last year, and about a man named Gabe."

Three days later, Beth's doctor and friend, Alan, and his wife joined Joe and Beth to witness their marriage. No other people attended the wedding. Joe and Beth wanted an intimate and private service.

Reverend Thomas stood before Joe and Beth and read from 1 Corinthians 13. When he finished, he said to Joe. "Take Beth's hands in yours and repeat after me. I, Joseph Zechariah, take you, Mary Elizabeth, to be my wife . . ."

A week later, the newlyweds arrived at the Asylum in Los Angeles. Ignoring Beth's protests, Joe carried her over the threshold and set her in the entryway.

"We're home," Joe called. Silence answered him. "Where is everybody?"

Joe checked the upstairs while Beth checked the living room. Not one boy could be found. "I told Jamal when we'd be arriving. I at least expected him to make sure the boys were here to greet you."

"Let's check in back," Beth suggested. "Maybe they're working in the yard."

"I'm sure we'd have heard them," Joe said. "If nothing else, they'd be listening to some music."

As Joe and Beth stepped into the backyard, they were met with whistles and cheers from the boys currently living at the house, but also from the boys who had lived with Joe from the beginning of the Asylum. Between the oak tree and the house stretched a huge banner with the words "Welcome home, Mom and Pops" and "Congratulations!" painted in fancy letters and wild colors. A three-tiered cake decorated with white frosting and red roses sat on one end of a table underneath the banner. At the other end of the table, sporting a large blue and pink bow, sat a wooden cradle with its own unique design carved into the end—the standard cross surrounded by a heart, but with the addition of the name "Connor" beneath it.

Beth traced the cross and heart and then the name with her finger, tears streaming down her cheeks as she did. Joe came up behind her and slipped his arms around her.

Her voice cracked. "Did you know they were going to do this?"

"No. It's as much a surprise to me as it is to you," Joe said. "It's beautiful. They must have worked extra hard to get it done by today."

Juan joined Joe and Beth at the table. "We figured you'd know from the cake and the banner that we're happy you and Pops are married," Juan said, a tentative smile forming as he spoke. "But we also wanted you to know we're happy about the baby, too." The rest of the boys came to stand beside and behind Juan. "Everyone chipped in time and money to make the cradle." he explained. "It's from all of us."

Beth wiped the wetness from her cheeks and smiled at Juan and the other boys, swallowing the lump forming in her throat. "It's the most precious gift I've ever received." She hugged Juan, whispering "thank you" as she did. And she hugged and thanked each boy in turn, her heart bursting with love.

~33~

December 30, 2014

Los Angeles, California

Gabe paced in front of the bank of television sets, awaiting the evening news. He hummed to himself, satisfied the events he witnessed over the last year had taken their proper course. One story—the one he should hear in a few minutes—would set into motion world-changing events. Gabe stopped pacing as the opening credits for the local news flashed on the screen.

"Good evening, and welcome to KABC News 7. I'm David Collins. Angela Hart will join us in a few moments.

"Our top news story this evening concerns the miracle birth we reported several days ago. As you will recall, we reported the birth of a healthy baby boy to a woman who had undergone a complete hysterectomy a little over six years ago. Doctors have been unable to explain why she was able to conceive and give birth to a healthy baby except to call the birth a miracle.

"Since we first reported the miracle, hundreds of people have flocked to the Sisters of Bethlehem Charity Hospital here in Los Angeles to celebrate the birth of this child. For a live report from the hospital grounds, here is Angela Hart. Angela."

"Thank you, David. I'm standing on the sidewalk in front of Bethlehem Charity Hospital, and as you can see behind me, hundreds of people are gathered on the lawn of the hospital. The people gathered here spend their time praying and singing hymns. Although most of the faces change from day to day, some of the faithful, as they call themselves, have been here from the beginning.

"One of those is Dr. Harold Evans, professor of religious studies at USC. Dr. Evans, can you tell me what is happening here?"

"What you're witnessing, Angela, is a prophecy come true. Those of us gathered here believe this miracle child is the one Father Lucas Ramirez predicted in his book *The Second Millennium and the Church.* We've come to celebrate the beginning of a new era of justice and peace for our world."

"Thank you Professor Evans. For those of you unfamiliar with Father Ramirez, he predicted a child would be born to a man of God and a barren woman and would bring justice, peace, and hope to the world. What you see behind me is the result of the belief that this prediction has taken place."

"Angela," David interrupted, "do we know the names of the parents?"

"No, David. At the request of the parents for privacy, the hospital refuses to release their names. We have confirmed, however, the father is a former Catholic priest, which certainly gives credence to Father Ramirez' prediction.

"This is Angela Hart, reporting live from Bethlehem Charity Hospital for KABC 7 News."

"Thank you, Angela. A hospital spokesman has reported that thousands of gifts have arrived daily at the hospital for the baby.

"When we return, we'll take you to Rome with news from the Vatican concerning the Pope's recent hospitalization, and an unusual phenomenon that has appeared recently in the night sky."

Gabe stuffed his hands in his pockets and jingled his change. One more news item, and he could move on. He listened eagerly through the remainder of the newscast. The final story made him smile.

"It seems to be the season for unusual phenomena. Astronomers at Mt. Wilson Observatory announced today the red giant star, Betelgeuse, located in the Orion constellation went supernova a few days ago. It was discovered when one of the astronomers at Mt. Wilson stepped outside to smoke a cigarette and saw a bright flash of light.

"Scientists are puzzled over the timing of the event. Their calculations predicted the red super giant would die slightly more than one million years from now. Betelgeuse is now the brightest star in the night sky and can easily be seen by the naked eye. Scientists will continue to study this event, hoping to find answers that will help them predict our own sun's evolution."

"It is done," Gabe whispered as he turned and walked away.

"There will be signs in the sun, moon, and stars."

Luke 21:25

". . . and a little child will lead them."

Isaiah 11:6

NOTE:

The incident of the star that went supernova is based on a true incident. An astronomer stepped outside for a cigarette and saw a bright flash. It was not the star Betelgeuse. The author used that particular star because it's the closest to going supernova of any of the other stars in our galaxy at the present time.

About the Author

K. L. (Karen) McKee has published a short story and written several articles and devotions for various publishers. She is a graduate of Regis University and worked as a Library Associate in the Reference Department of her county library for twenty-nine years. She is a member of Rocky Mountain Fiction Writers.

Karen lives in Western Colorado with her husband, Steve. She enjoys knitting, music—playing and singing—tennis, enjoying the beautiful outdoors of Western Colorado, and spending time with her family.

Made in the USA
Charleston, SC
21 April 2016

9R00137